Schlock

Editor: Ga

This month's cove
Meseguer from *Pixabc*
Gavin Chappell, logo aesign © by C Priest Brumley.

SCHLOCK! WEBZINE

Welcome to Schlock! the webzine for science fiction, fantasy, and horror.

Vol. 16, Issue 9
October 2020

Schlock! is a monthly webzine dedicated to short stories, flash fiction, serialised novels, and novellas, within the genres of science fiction, fantasy, and horror. We publish new and old works of pulp sword and sorcery, urban fantasy, dark fantasy, and gothic horror. If you want to read quality works of new pulp fantasy, science fiction or horror, Schlock! is the webzine for you!

For details of previous editions, please go to the website.

Schlock! Webzine is always willing to consider new science fiction, fantasy and horror short stories, serials, graphic novels and comic strips, reviews and art. Submit fiction, articles, art, or links to your own site to editor@schlock.co.uk. We no longer review published and self-published novels directly, although we are willing to accept reviews from other writers.

Any other enquiries also to editor@schlock.co.uk

ISBN: 9798691109065

This month, a chef becomes morbidly fascinated by a repellent new employee. The army is called in on Picklock Lane after a terrifying new discovery. A new drive-in is in town, but the films it shows are out-of-this-world. The master tailor of Hedgeville has a strange new commission for the local sculptor. And Lu makes the lamentable mistake of buying a new scooter on Halloween.

Kassi, alone, reaches the edge of the desert. Candace is visited by an ominous red crow. A cowardly lieutenant discovers there are worse horrors than the front line. Nadja tells Robert why her pubic hair is blue. And Art is blown into a strange new dimension.

Meanwhile, the Florentine Vampire remembers the vampire who bit him. And finally, Ted gets on with the job.

Gavin Chappell

Vincent is an artist who has consistently been on assignment in the art world for over twenty years. Throughout his career he has acquired a toolbox of diverse skills (from freehand drawing to digital design, t shirt designer to muralist). His styles range from the wildly abstract to pulp style comics. In 2013, his work in END TIMES won an award in the Best Horror Anthology category for that year. When Vincent is not at his drawing board he can be found in the classroom teaching cartooning and illustration to his students at Westchester Community College in Valhalla NY. He lives in Mamaroneck NY with his wife Jennie and dog Skip.

https://www.freelanced.com/vincentdavis

DONOVAN'S ERROR by Mathew Roy Davey

There was something about Donovan Lear that intrigued Chef de Partie, Andrew Woodhouse, from the off. Both were smokers and Woodhouse made sure they took their coffee breaks at the same time. Lear was flattered and confused by the attention.

Woodhouse watched Lear as he scrubbed away at stubborn sauce marks on crockery and pans, fascinated and repelled by his reptilian presence. He noted the waitresses avoiding the new man despite him doing nothing to justify their aversion.

After a couple of days, Woodhouse was giving Lear lifts to and from work, careful not to let his colleagues see them arrive or depart together. No one else spoke with Lear so there was little chance of anyone finding out. Lear lived in a crummy flat near the canal. Woodhouse hadn't once seen anyone around during the pickup or drop-off. Lear seemed to be the only resident of the whole run-down district.

The other chefs mocked Lear, and Woodhouse joined them in the teasing. Lear would smile at him, hoping he might be in on the jokes he usually failed to understand. The others noticed the smiles and joked there was a sexual frisson going on. Woodhouse laughed along.

Woodhouse, Woodlouse to his colleagues, began probing Lear, discussing drugs, pornography, seeing what Lear would disclose, encouraging him when he showed interest in anything remotely deviant. Lear, desperate to impress and failing to see the duplicity of his new friend, so unused was he to intimacy, soon revealed he had beaten to death a young barmaid who had spurned his advances. Lear had hidden in the toilets when she'd been closing up and attacked her when everyone else had gone. He'd bundled her body into the broom closet and left. He'd been arrested within twenty four hours.

Woodhouse was impressed. He'd not expected such a revelation. He'd been expecting some sort of sex crime, child molestation or rape. Lear, he discovered, had served ten years before being granted parole. This was his first job.

Having always been interested in killing, Woodhouse quizzed Lear about the crime and was both thrilled and sickened by the fire in Lear's eyes as he recounted and relived the young woman's last moments. Woodhouse had always wondered what it would be like to take another's life, and in Lear he saw an opportunity.

One evening, on the way home from a shift, he stopped the car and suggested they smoke a joint by the canal. Woodhouse did not inhale a great deal but watched as Lear grew glassy-eyed. When Lear leaned over and tried to kiss him, any concerns over conscience left Woodhouse completely. He pushed Lear over on his side and bashed his head on the kerbstone until he heard a crunch. Glancing around, he then rolled Lear into the canal where he floated face down and drifted away.

When the body was recovered the next day it was presumed that he'd slipped and fallen in. Toxicology tests confirmed this. The police didn't even interview Woodhouse.

It was so easy it wasn't long before he started wondering how he might do something similar again...

LOVECRAFTIANA

THE MAGAZINE OF ELDRITCH HORROR

INCENSE OF IREM

Lee Clark Zumpe

THE LOST ARCHIVIST

David Kenney

PLUS CTHULHUVIAN POETRY
from Matthew Wilson
and Sandro D. Fossemò

VOLUME FOUR ISSUE TWO

LAMMAS EVE 2019

SKY HIGH MAYBE by EW Farnsworth

On Picklock Lane, traffic had been reduced to a single lane, and the machinery for removing large portions of cobblestones and paving had worked all morning to clear the way for an unusual work gang in white scientific jackets to commence. Rumours abounded about the disruption. The phalanxes of yellow press persons had been told by their editors to look elsewhere for their hot stories. Something was Hush-Hush, for certain.

Fatty sat at his usual table in the tavern, nursing his pint and listening to the speculations of Miriam Uber, whose husband happened to be one of the white-coated gentlemen who had entered the grey tent overhanging the secret labour beneath the street.

"Sheriff, it's just not fair. I'm the man's wife, God Bless him. You should think I, of all people, have the right to know what's happening down there. Miles was an explosives expert in Afghanistan, but he's home now. Do you know anything at all?"

Fatty shook his head. "Mrs. Periwinkle, I know nothing. And if I did—not saying I do, mind you—I probably couldn't tell you even knowing who you are. A complete blackout has been laid over the goings-on. When it's over, I'm sure the authorities will let us know in the usual way."

"I'll just have another pint." She raised her plump hand, and the barkeep nodded. "I have the jitters just thinking about poor Miles. They called him at four o'clock this morning and told him to bring his full kit-bag of war goodies and tools with him. That's never happened before. I've been running his stories about being in the sand. He won't talk about his sapper duties with IEDs, the improvised explosive devices. My spine gets chills running up and down when I think of those nasty bombs."

"Mrs. Periwinkle, I'm afraid I really cannot help you. I've purposely not asked about the digging. As sheriff, I only care about keeping the peace in the meantime. Here's your new pint. Drink up. It will all be over soon. Then your husband can tell you all about it. If, that is, he is permitted to do so."

"So what he is doing is classified. Why didn't you just say so? My Lands!" she drank a deep draught and wiped her upper lip with her monogrammed handkerchief. She then munched on a biscuit. Her eyes roamed around the room. She spotted one of her gossips entering the front door. She beamed and rose, taking her pint with her without saying goodbye.

Fatty shrugged. Something about the woman's prattle revolved in his fertile brain. He stood and made his way to the entrance. He walked down the lane to the tent and peered into the opening. No one was inside the tent at the street level, but he could hear whispers coming from the hole the men had made earlier in the day.

"Past. That's an old one. My guess is late 1940. It's clear it never exploded."

"That doesn't mean it couldn't explode any second."

"Damn! I wish I had a third hand. No thank you. I don't want your mitt in my line of sight. It's hard enough for me to see with the little light I've got."

The sheriff slipped down the rope ladder past the three men who were looking over the round metal object.

"Good morning, Sheriff."

"Is you name Miles Periwinkle, by chance?"

"That's me all right. I've been given charge of making this monster safe."

"You said you needed a third hand?"

"Not likely I'll grow one just like that." He snapped his free fingers by way of illustration. Fatty saw that the area around the bomb was wet from the water line that had been the original reason for the hole dug around it. The crew had found the round explosive while they were digging around the pipe. Fortunately, one of the workers recognized what they had found.

"Just out of curiosity, where would you want that extra hand to be put?"

"It's that I have to use two hands to steady and turn this wrench. Over there is the detonator, and I'd like to have something between the two points you see right there." He shone his torch on the leads. "I don't expect what I'm doing with the wrench will dislodge the bomb, but if it did, the two blocks all around this point would be totally demolished. Everyone would be killed."

The other two workmen became pale and backed off. Fatty's eyes narrowed. "Seeing as you two can't help, why don't you go up the ladder to the nearest pub? Have a few while we two take care of this situation. But mind you, don't say a word. If I ever discover you mentioned a bomb was down here, I'll skin you alive."

The two men did as the sheriff ordered. Meanwhile, Fatty was getting technical details about the bomb from Miles.

"The Krauts knew their business. Why this bomb was a dud, I don't know. It has been sitting here waiting for someone to find it since the Battle of Britain. It just goes to show that nothing is ever over for good."

"All right, Miles, let's go 'easy does it.' I want to help you, but I don't want to make a silly mistake that will blow us all sky high maybe. Don't worry about how I'm going to manage it, but I won't get in there with you to crowd you. I'll place my appendage between the two leads you showed me. If I get the placement wrong, you can help me adjust."

Miles kept working with his wrench. He seemed to be conscious that the sheriff was now touching the place between the two leads of the detonator. He shook his head.

"Is anything wrong?"

"So you're one of them."

"And your point is?"

"Use that thing to keep the two leads apart no matter what happens. Is there any way you could wrap one of your suckers around each of those leads simultaneously?"

Fatty adjusted his tentacle and arranged his suckers accordingly. "How am I doing?"

"Just fine. As I turn this wrench, those leads are going to try to snap together. You must not let metal touch metal."

"I have the picture. Turn the cock when you are ready."

Miles pulled with maximum torque and leverage. The earth that held the bomb in place remained tight as a glove. The leads did try to close, but Fatty's tentacles kept them from touching. The tentacle was pinched so hard that the sheriff said, "Ouch. That hurt!"

Miles was smiling now. "It does not hurt as much as

the bomb would have done."

"I guess not. Anyway, are we safe now?"

"The cock is out, and the leads have become fastened—with your suckers keeping the metal pieces from meeting. I'm going up to report what we've done. The bomb squad will help me raise the safed bomb to the truck—all under the tent so no one will panic. Do you think you can keep the passers-by from craning their necks?"

"I'll get my tentacle free and go up to the street level. You go right ahead and report your business. I'll think of something to tell the press."

"You can show them this coin." Miles handed Fatty a five-reichsmark coin. "Tell them we found a treasure trove buried by English spies for the day the Krauts intended to invade."

"Hm. That might cover a multitude of sins."

"Speaking of which, is your tentacle going to heal?"

"If it does not heal, I'll just grow another." Fatty had pulled his tentacle free. A ribbon of his flesh remained between the leads. "Also—I'd appreciate your not letting on what happened down here."

"Who would believe me if I told? I don't believe it myself." He shook his head. Miles then disappeared up the ladder. Fatty clambered up after him, after he had stuffed his wounded appendage back under his shirt.

By the time Miles returned with the workmen and their explosives disposal truck, the sheriff was busy directing traffic. He would wave the southbound traffic through. Then he would stop that flow and let the opposite traffic flow. He showed a patrolman what he was doing. Then he helped align the truck and the winch-driven chain that would raise the bomb. Miles, the subject matter expert, knew how to lift out a bomb. Within an hour, the huge weapon was on the truck. A tarp was tied over it. The truck drove away, with Miles riding shotgun and waving at Fatty.

The rest of the road show was mechanical. By sundown, the water pipe was fixed, the road had been patched, and Fatty was back in the pub nursing a new pint. Mrs. Periwinkle was ecstatic.

"Sheriff, you were away for all the action."

"What action, Mrs. Periwinkle?"

"Two workmen came in and sat at your table. They came at me from both sides when I sat down with my gossip. They pinched my bottom from both sides simultaneously. Imagine that!"

"Did your gossip witness this outrage?"

"Witness it? They pinched her bottom too."

"So are you going to make a formal complaint?"

"And ruin my reputation? Not on your life."

"What about your gossip?"

"She knows what's what, I can tell you."

"So the upshot of all this hanky-panky is what?"

"I just wanted to let you know what goes on right under your nose when you aren't paying attention. Speaking of which, I found out what my hubby was doing down in the sewer."

"I'm all ears, Mrs. Periwinkle. But don't tell me anything your husband would not want you to divulge."

"Well, while you were away, my Miles was trying to secure a chest full of Nazi money. Imagine finding loot from eighty years ago under Pickwick Lane in a broken sewer! Why they called my husband in when they should have called a numismatist, I'll never know."

"These are strange times, Mrs. Periwinkle."

13

"Are you in pain, Sheriff?"

"Nothing time won't heal, Ma'am."

"Well, this has been a day to remember. Now that the sewer and the lane have been fixed, it will seem as if nothing happened today at all. But we'll know differently, won't we, Sheriff?"

"I guess so. Have a good rest of your day."

The portly lady sidled up to Fatty's right ear and whispered, "I wouldn't want it to get around, but my Miles said something weird happened while he was under the lane. An enormous octopus swam up in the sewer and volunteered to help my husband with the pelf."

Fatty whispered, "And what happened then?"

"Miles was too polite to refuse the creature. He let the octopus help and in repayment for his kindness, he gave the octopod the chest of Nazi coins. That was so like my Miles. Of course, now he won't be able to prove that any of his story is true. That's the way of the world we live in, isn't it, Sheriff?"

"If you say so, Mrs. Periwinkle. It was good having a pint with you today."

"Don't worry about me, Sheriff. I won't breathe a word about what really went down. That will remain a secret between my husband, you and my gossip."

It was seven o'clock before Fatty could get to his doctor's office. He had called her to remain open to see him. She examined his wounded tentacle and pronounced his wounds as superficial. "I don't suppose you're going to tell me what happened to your suckers today?"

"That matter is highly confidential. I'm just concerned that my tentacle will heal eventually."

"It will be as right as rain in a week or so. If it does not heal, come back. In the worst case, I could amputate. I see that you're pained by that thought. We are hardier than we know, Sheriff."

Fatty thanked his doctor and offered her cash for services rendered, but she refused. "I have to keep careful accounting, or I'll be arrested by the likes of you and jailed for aeons. Tell me it's not so."

The sheriff elected to be silent. He walked home and found his clones busy with all the sundry activities of his many enterprises. Though he was trammelled with quotidian functions during the daylight hours, at night he was absorbed in his criminal activities. He found the five-reichsmark coin in his pocket and flipped it into the air. It came up heads, he thought. He decided to keep the token. After all, the yellow press was likely to ask him what he was doing while the lane was torn up all day. The coin would keep the newshounds off his case.

As for the wild stories Mrs. Periwinkle and her gossip were spreading, those old wives' tales belonged in the tavern where they had originated. Fatty thought for a moment about what might have happened if his tentacle had not intervened today in Miles Periwinkle's assistance, but he quickly suppressed the idea. Where on Earth would he find a better venue than his own pub on his own Picklock Lane within easy walking distance of his home sweet home?

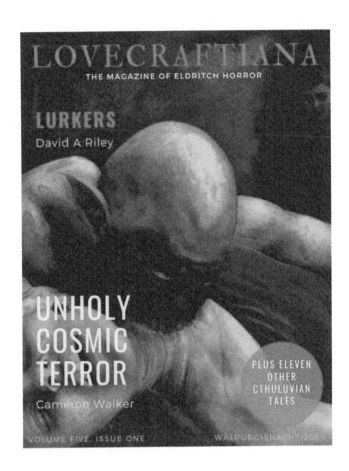

LOVECRAFTIANA

THE MAGAZINE OF ELDRITCH HORROR

LURKERS
David A Riley

UNHOLY COSMIC TERROR
Cameron Walker

PLUS ELEVEN OTHER CTHULUVIAN TALES

VOLUME FIVE, ISSUE ONE

WALPURGISNACHT 2020

THE DRIVE-IN FROM HELL by Carlton Herzog

Jason Scott and Ricky Clemons were a pair of quirky film fanatics who had a dream: they wanted to revive the Old Trenton Drive-In Movie Theatre on Olden Avenue. But they couldn't come up with the cash to purchase a digital projector. So, they opted to bring the Theatre back to life by screening vintage 35mm film prints and working entirely for free.

The two of them knew nothing of Trenton, let alone the history of the Drive-in. Because it sat adjacent to several hellish dimensions, people in the know referred to Trenton variously as the Jaws of Hell, the Crack of Doom, and the Devil's Throat. It is rumoured that Durer's woodcuts and many of Hieronymus Bosch's paintings—along with those of a certain AJ Pickman—were inspired by dramatic visions of the real Trenton.

Not surprisingly, Trenton had been the home of several satanic churches that were later razed by the citizenry. Even before those formal institutions of evil had arisen, covens of witches had called Trenton home. They too were purged by burnings and beheadings, but not before they inflicted many plagues upon the locals.

To be sure, the good people of Trenton had done their best to rid the land of Satan's scourge. Trenton's diabolical leanings did not disappear entirely. Rather, they went underground or were channelled into more respectable enterprises. Sid Samhain, for example, ran an antique shop on Broad Street. As Sid's surname suggests, he had more than a passing knowledge of occult matters. So, while much of his inventory was of the quotidian variety suitable for traditional collectors, he also reserved a section of the shop for his special customers—an assortment of witches, warlock, sorcerers and the occasional incarnated demon.

He carried an extensive collection of 35mm film prints. Some were garden variety old movies going back as far as the silent ones from the early twentieth century. Others were accursed, having received hell's imprimatur to wreak as much havoc in the world as possible. The films did this in one of two ways: either the movie patron was sucked into the screen and became an unwilling part of the story, or the characters in the film came to life, walked off the screen and worked their mischief in the theatre and its environs.

Although Jason and Ricky had found Sid to be affable as well as eccentric, they were oblivious to his dark side and that of his inventory. Hence, Sid was the logical source for any and all 35mm film needs from the outset. Moreover, his shop was close to the theatre and his prices surprisingly reasonable, almost as if he wanted to give the films away without seeming to do so.

Jason and Ricky wanted to open the Drive-In in dramatic fashion. They intended to offer a double feature of an obscure horror film from the 30's: WHAT FIENDS MAY COME. They advertised the event on local radio and television shows, put up makeshift billboards, told family and friends, and at one point even rode around town with a P.A. system announcing the event.

When the fateful night came, Ricky worked the ticket booth, while Jason manned the projector. So great was the turnout that cars were lined up for a quarter mile waiting to get in. There was a large sign outside the drive-in that said that there were not enough people to operate the concession stand, echoing what had already ben promulgated by various means of public announcement. Patrons could, however, bring along their own food and drink, but alcohol, in theory, was banned.

The film opened to Wagner's Ride of the Valkyries. That was followed by a brief crackling prologue playing out on grainy celluloid:

How do you do. Before we begin, the producers believe it fair to offer a word of warning about the story that is about to unfold. It's about that greatest of mysteries the human psyche and the monsters that lurk deep within it. It may thrill you; it may shock you; it will most certainly horrify you. So, if you have a weak constitution and are likely to be disturbed by such things, we urge you leave now. You have been warned.

The crowd tingled with excitement. Not simply because of the Drive-In's resurrection. But also, because no one in the audience, including Jason and Ricky, had ever heard of, let alone seen the film before.

Jason continued running the projector. Ricky, for his part, sat on the hood of his car mesmerized by the film. He smoked cigarette after cigarette as the action unfolded.

The story involved a doctor by the name of Arthur Machen who wanted to perform surgery that would open his patients' minds to supernatural vistas where they would see the Great God Pan. The medical community regarded his experiments as quackery. Unable to find a willing volunteer, Doctor Machen, with the help of his trusted footman, William, ply a local drunk, Tom Bottom, with laudanum and liquor. They bring him back to the doctor's laboratory and perform the surgery on the now unconscious man.

When the man wakes up, he can remember nothing of the night before, nor even who he is. He does relate that he sees through the world around him—beyond the veil of this reality—into others. He says that he can see Nodens, god of the deep abyss.

Doctor Machen keeps the man under observation so he can study the effects of the surgery. He goes out to dinner with some colleagues. On his return he finds that his footman William has been gruesomely murdered, and Tom Bottom is nowhere to be found.

As the days pass, there are a series of unexplained murders in London. Doctor Machen suspects his erstwhile patient is responsible but is afraid to tell the police. So, he arms himself and goes in search of the murderer.

William, who is something of a classicist, tells Doctor Machen that "there may be more than one. As I recall from the Nonnus' *Dionysiaca*—the story of Dionysius in India—Pan could be multiplied into a swarm of Pans. In that epic, Pan had 12 sons. His influence therefore is like a virus that can spread. The goat of a thousand young."

At this point in the movie Jason sees a superimposed satyr on the screen. It's not part of the movie. It seems to be talking to him directly, but Jason can't understand what he is saying. He gets off his car and walks up to the screen. He touches it and feels a slight tingling. He can feel himself changing. His body starts sprouting hair everywhere. Large horns grow from his head, and he now has the hindquarters and legs of a goat.

But his supernatural transformation is only one of

many. He looks around and sees other satyrs leaving their cars and cavorting around the grounds. He suddenly feels the urge to eat raw meat. He spots an untransformed couple in a convertible and bounds towards them. Before they can do anything, he tears into the throat of the young man behind the wheel. He alternately gulps blood and chews flesh as the woman paralyzed with fright just stares at the tableau in horror.

That scene is being repeated throughout the drive-in as a multitude of Pans emerge from otherwise normal people. There is a panic as some flee on foot and others drive away.

For his part, Ricky has been watching the movie and not paying attention to what was happening with the audience. He was focused on changing the reels over at just the right time. It was at one of those moments that he came out of his cinematic fog and realized what was happening. He tried calling Jason but got no answer.

Ricky shut down the projector, but it was too late. Hell's hand had reached up from the abyss and grabbed his everyday world by the throat. It had no intention of letting go just yet. He didn't know what to do other than lock the projection booth and hope that things would calm down. But judging from the screams that might take a while.

The projector hadn't been shut down very long before it restarted itself. He pulled the plug and it ran anyway. By now the story on the screen showed that the police and Doctor Machen had cornered Tom Bottom in an alleyway. That should have been the end of the movie as the fiend got his just deserts.

But then the Pans at the drive-in began stepping into the movie as easily as you or I would walk into another room. They descended on the constables and tore them apart. Then they along with Tom Bottom, who was dragging the good Doctor with him, jumped back off the screen and began ravaging the remaining patrons in the drive-in.

Ricky smashed the projector with a chair. Although he knocked it to the booth floor, it kept playing. He smacked it again and again with the chair, all to no effect.

He tried to pick it up and smash it on the floor, but it was hot to the touch and burned his hand. He then tried jamming a screwdriver into the reel. But the reel cut through the screwdriver like a hot knife through butter and kept on spinning.

Ricky heard a soft knock at the door. It was Jason.

"Come on, man, open up. It's not safe out here for me."

Ricky was on the horns of a dilemma. That was the normal voice of his friend, but his friend had transformed before his eyes into a bloodthirsty fiend.

"Dude, I'm sorry. I can't do that."

"Please open up."

"Man, go look at yourself in a mirror. You're a monster who's here to eat me."

That last bit of dialogue was followed by a bloodcurdling, angry scream. Ricky nearly wet his pants.

Jason was pounding on the door. The sounds he made were those of a feral beast, not Ricky's friend Jason.

Had Ricky turned his attention to the screen, he would have seen that the newly created Pans were dragging the remaining drive-in patrons back into the movie screen and then killing them as part of the movie. But his attention was on barring the door against the fiend on the other side of it.

He hit upon the idea of climbing out the projection window. That was followed by a bit of fiery inspiration when he looked down and saw the full can of paint thinner. He figured that if he could get out the window and get above whatever Jason had become, he could douse it with the thinner and then set it on fire. Toasting goat boy seemed the only viable means of escape.

So, he grabbed the thinner, made sure his lighter worked, quietly clambered out the window, and stood on top of the booth. He crawled to edge and peeked over to find what was once Jason clawing and licking the door while making mewling sounds like a goat in heat. He watched in fascination.

He slowly unscrewed the cap to the thinner and then dumped it on the satyr. It fumed and growled. The smell of the thinner both confused and infuriated it. But before it could clear its eyes to see the source of its irritation, Ricky dropped a burning rag onto it, and the beast lit up like a human torch.

Ricky could smell its hair and flesh burning together with the acrid stink of the thinner. The thing ran in insane circles, shrieking and spitting. As it did, Ricky eased himself off the booth. He ran for the exit. Before he did, he looked back to see the pan thing run to the movie screen and onto the screen still on fire.

He realized that he was the only one alive in the drive-in. Everyone else had joined the feature presentation. So, he stopped running and watched the remainder of the movie.

By now, Doctor Machen and William had found

themselves surrounded by a swarm of Pans comprised largely of the transformed drive-in movie-goers. The movie ended with the swarm closing in on the two, followed by a larger scene of pandemonium at large from a multitude of Pans overrunning cities around the world. Then the screen faded to black.

Ricky felt that the gruesome affair was over. But there was still the matter of that cursed film. He headed back to the projection booth which was now on fire. The burning Pan had inadvertently set the dilapidated structure ablaze when it bumped into it during its frenzy. Ricky stood there and watched it burn down to that last glowing ember.

After the fire subsided, he picked through the ashes to see if the film had been destroyed. It had not. Although the projector was burned, blackened and melted, the film was untouched by the flames.

Ricky didn't want to leave it there. Somebody else might find it and replay the gruesome drama in the streets of Trenton. He reached for it and found it cool to the touch.

He took it back to Sid's.

Sid asked, "So was it everything you thought it would be?"

"You knew all along, didn't you?"

"I had some idea but wasn't clear on the specifics."

"I'm out of the 35mm movie business. From now on, I'll stick to digital shorts on You-tube."

"Is that so? In that case, I have a digital camera you're sure to love. It was once owned by the horror film maker Johnny Abbadon. It has an eternal life battery, so it never needs charging."

"Sounds insidious."

"Oh, it is. Just you point it at yourself, and you'll be an Internet Star."

"How much?"

"For you, Superstar, it's free."

"Free?"

"I represent a consortium that wants to invest in your future. We see you have unlimited growth potential. So, take the camera for now and get started. We'll get back to you with a contract."

"Sound too good to be true."

"It is."

UNVEILING by James Moran

In his thirty-ninth year the master tailor of Hedgeville began to sense the delicious presence of something powerful all around him.

The sense began as a notion that somewhere nearby lingered an old friend he'd completely forgotten about. In the marketplace he'd taken to slowing down and backing up to poke his head around alleyways he'd just turned down.

Though the presence was shadowy and mysterious he was never scared. He was excited. He'd led a lonely life. His parents had expired, and his work had been his only comfort. Now this presence had come, seemingly cut from his own cloth, yet continually increasing in yardage and capable of protecting him from every imaginable element.

Within two months of first catching its scent he recognized it all around him, in everything. For twenty years he'd beat up and down the same commons every spring without once recognizing that every tree, bush, and blade of grass was indeed that powerful presence. The same went for those familiar warty, hacking faces he passed in the market. Skin was merely an outfit beneath an outfit worn by that very power which swelled to bursting on all sides of the master tailor every moment of his workday. If only those faces could be convinced of what they clothed.

For the past three years the master tailor had met twice a year at Tully's Tavern in Hempsmead with Gavin Greyhound, the metalsmith turned sculptor. Each year Greyhound had been commissioned to create a sculpture—first a bust, then the full figure of a duke, then the prince on a horse. And each year they'd met over brunch, griped at odds with each other about the bill, eventually splitting it down to coppers, and worked out a subcommission for a piece of dark canvas to cover the sculpture until its unveiling.

This year was no different. Slumped behind a bowl of lamb stew, Greyhound had brought along his usual dark cloud. Only this time, he wouldn't speak. He grumbled and shifted about.

The tailor watched intently and sipped his stew.

"Right then, thing is," said Greyhound, "I've got another job. Big one. Thing is, I'll need twice the yardage at only two thirds the budget."

"I'm sure we can work something out."

Greyhound screwed up his face like he'd tasted something bad. "What's your angle?"

"My angle is I'll have to see what you've completed of the commission immediately or two thirds the budget won't work for me."

"Why's that?"

"Because it's two-thirds the budget."

"Why do you need to see it then?"

"I don't need to see anything."

"I hardly have sketches right now."

The tailor gathered his coat.

"I hardly have an armature."

"That will be sufficient to prove the scope of the commission."

"What's the matter with you?"

"Don't work with me if something's the matter with me."

Greyhound grumbled and gathered his coat.

At this the tailor tossed a handful of coins on the table

and had hardly turned to go when Greyhound's hot breath was in his ear. "Are you trying to make a fool out of me?"

"Only if you're trying to make a fool of me." He wove out of the tavern then offered Greyhound the lead.

Shortly, they approached an old stable. Greyhound unlocked the enormous doors and pulled one open.

"Your foundry?" the tailor asked.

Greyhound grunted a confirmation. That was all the tailor needed.

As soon as Greyhound placed a foot over the threshold, the tailor charged, banging the door closed with Greyhound caught in the gap. The blow stunned Greyhound. The tailor charged again, smashing Greyhound between the doors. He charged a third time and didn't bother looking about for witnesses. The power protected him. No one would see.

Greyhound collapsed inside the threshold of the foundry. He moaned. He was barely conscious.

The tailor pulled his shears from his jacket and went to work. Without removing Greyhound's wool sweater and shirt, he palpated the sculptor's belly button, then pierced it with the lower blade of the shears and slid them up past the sculptor's sternum to his collarbone as if cutting three lengths of cloth at once.

A year later Gavin Greyhound unveiled the sculpture that he would be remembered for. This unveiling was not a conventional one, the crowd quickly came to realize. The veil over the enormous statue was not a veil at all, for it was made of bronze. It was an essential part of a sculpture of a man struggling against that very veil, pulling at it, arching his sinuous body to tear himself free of it.

The master tailor of Hempsmead had since disappeared and was never seen again.

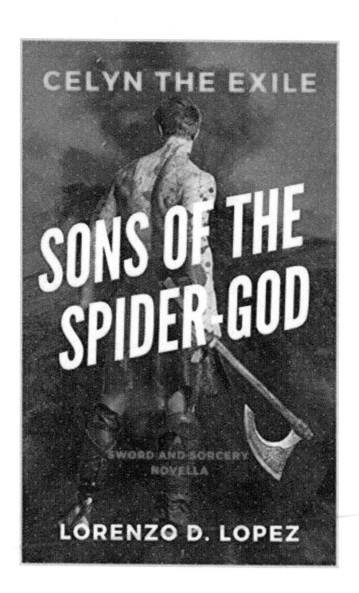

CELYN THE EXILE

SONS OF THE SPIDER-GOD

A SWORD AND SORCERY
NOVELLA

LORENZO D. LOPEZ

I BOUGHT A VAMPIRE MOPED by GK Murphy

When Lu saw her new scooter in the barn of farmer Giles Dullard, on the outskirts of town, she knew it was the moped for her, without any shadow of a doubt—instantly the chemistry was established, she knew, the farmer knew, the bike knew. Figuratively, this unique partnership would serve to form a tight bond, forged equally in wanton desire, love, obsession, style and this vehicle's flawless gleaming chrome, to engender what might have soon became an ungodly union between mere human and road machine. It would surpass any desire Lu had experienced before. After all, this raw anomaly was something she had simply fallen in love with amid a sudden unexpected wave, combined with a certain fervent lust, and all this for the very first time in her meek twenty-one years on the planet.

The young Korean woman had lived with her girlfriend Emily until they argued one night and Emily walked out never to return. It bothered neither, for as folk often said there were plenty of other fish in the sea and Emily certainly wasn't the first, nor would she be the last…who needed rules, right?

Giles Dullard stroked his scruffy grey goatee and mumbled incoherently. With his thick moustache entering his mouth and lack of teeth, the 78 year old farmer was a picture to behold, but a wise and weathered one at that, with obvious and greater life experience than the 21 year old college student seeking to purchase her first means of transport.

Lu said, "It looks in perfect shape for a ten year old scooter. But what it the dent on the front bit? I mean, don't get me wrong, Mr Dullard, I'm interested in buying, but I need answers to certain questions, otherwise I might be making a huge mistake."

"The knock came from my brother Jake's head. Shortly afterwards, he went and suddenly died in hospital after some time on a ventilator. You see, miss, Jake lost an awful lot of blood and his brains were leaking out of his ear sockets."

Lu couldn't quite believe her own ears. But she remained steadfast and undeterred.

"I think some of his blood might still be on it. God, what a tale...somebody could write a horror story about it, I bet."

Dullard chuckled. He turned his eyes to the greying skies this Sunday afternoon and squinted as he said, "Halloween tomorrow night... lots of horror stories about Halloween. Jake passed away last Halloween, due to his accident of course... his accident with Alexandra."

"Who is Alexandra, sir... his girlfriend?"

Dullard looked at Lu like she was a lunatic and the question was insane. "You're looking at Alex, miss. Alex is the bike's name!"

There was a silence.

However, for Lu, there was also something was magical and romantic about all this.

"I have the two hundred pounds you are asking, Mr Dullard. I've passed my CBT and have my Provisional Licence, so I can just drive her away."

"Alex will only cost you a fiver a week on petrol, miss. She might bog every five miles or so—bog—you know—splutter a bit—but nothing to worry about, just ride it out and she'll be fine."

Lu had heard this before, mostly concerning motorcycles. She said, "I'm not buying a casualty, am I, sir?"

"Alex has twelve months' MOT. If she had issues, she wouldn't have sailed through that MOT."

It made perfect sense. Lu handed Giles Dullard the notes in exchange for two sets of keys.

"When are you taking her on the road?" Dullard asked, adding, "She's quite possessive, but treat her right and she'll treat you right."

Alex was black with beige leather seat. The bike looked almost new.

"Tomorrow night, I'm going to a Halloween party across town. I can't wait to show Judy."

"…Judy?"

"Oh, she's a girl I like. In fact, I really fancy her!"

Dullard seemed to smile amid the oily beard. "Ah, so you like to jam with the bearded clam, eh?"

Taking no offence, Lu enthused, "Yeah, she'll be so jealous. She'll have competition for my affections and attention. I know she'll love Alex…"

Lu boarded the scooter and revved her up. It was the sweetest sound ever.

Shortly, she was motoring away from the farm and up the hill leading towards town, and what started as a sunny day had become cold and grey.

In the distant skies over the Cumbrian hills, sinister figures and faces seemed to appear in the black clouds, hiding away the sun, their grotesque floating shadows contorted and twisted with what appeared from a distance to be like anguish or the most terrible pain. Some of the clouds seemed to have glaring eyes, some with eyes like black pinpoints, narrowed and squinting. They seemed to stare and curse all beneath in the valleys and townships of the Lake District.

Lu slept uneasily and alone in the bedroom of her flat that night. The scooter outside in the back yard plagued her dreams, turning them into obscene nightmares, ones where she saw doomed Jake Dullard, with his brains seeping from his lugholes, dripping onto his shoulders and down his front, as he grinned perversely, his teeth yellow and green. It was like the joke she heard about teeth. "Summer Teeth... some are yellow, some are green..." But nothing was funny about these particular dreams. Amid them, Jake's face was everywhere, mostly between her legs, whilst Lu felt his rancid breath against her crotch, his tongue arched and piercing her white cotton panties.

When she woke, it was ten past midnight... five minutes into Halloween and already she felt the true spirit of the festival.

It was cold outside but no wind or even the slightest breeze.

The country was gripped by Covid-19 and leaving the European Union. Which she had long since stopped caring about... these would always be there, especially this frightful virus nobody understood and constantly played down, as a population lied to itself and bypassed common sense, in the end seemingly holding each other under the water...

Suddenly, in the cold darkness of the bedroom, Lu heard a noise and hurriedly reached for the bedside lamp. She quickly switched it on. Lu realized with a panic that her nightmare continued, as well as acknowledging that she was not alone in the room. There was a hum, a steady burr... it sounded like a bike engine turning over. However, how could that be? After all, she was in a room two storeys up in the apartment block on

Whitehaven harbour, so how could it be? Also, where was that VILE LAUGHTER coming from…?

The front of the bike had long sharp teeth and it grinned maniacally as blood and bile drooled from its mouth and dripped onto the laminated wooden floor. This created a thick scarlet pool under its axis and wheels. This monstrosity, obscenely called by a sweet innocent name as Alexandra, was now something like a mechanical creature similar to a vampire—seemed to grin from the foot of the bed where it was stationed with a figure on top, yet also appeared vicious and bloodthirsty, a machine which sought her death, and craved her blood and youthful flesh.

The obscene and withered figure of the ghostly Jake Dullard did nothing except grin idiotically from astride the burring demonic black vehicle, his brains leaking from cracks in the bone and spilling out from minor cavities in his fragmented, rotten skull. A stunned Lu was unable to so much as even mumble or mutter—never mind the impossibly inability to open her mouth to speak—for she was understandably too petrified to even move, since she was locked in a peculiar state of stock-stillness, as a desperate muted anxiety and fearfulness overtook her.

"No, no please, please no…" she managed as gravity took control and she experienced her body in the motions and revolutions of being sucked towards Alexandra, and in particular that widening, toothy, gaping mouth, as the mechanical nightmare gnashed and drooled, clacking both sets of teeth hungrily. Before unfortunate Lu knew it, her lower body was in its mouth and about to be crushed.

She screamed for the final time before the mouth

clamped shut with a loud snap. Blood squirted and sprayed everywhere from her ripped flesh, as her one definitive scream proved final and short-lived.

Some way, through the bothersome chewing of its prey, the metallic vampire paused as if to catch its breath amid the slurping of blood and chomping on flesh and crunching of bone. The beast onboard, Jake Dullard, was the reason for this. The eating and movement had suddenly stopped and there was stillness in the room. Outside the window, another heavy wave of rain had resumed and a huge roaring wind had picked up. A cold October night, nothing special there for Cumbria...

Something was brewing in this room.

Jake leaned forward on the beige leather scooter seat, seeming to whisper into the protruding right-hand mirror, almost like it was an ear.

Simply, he said, "Happy Halloween, Alexandra!"

KASSI AND THE EDGE OF THE DESERT by Ste Whitehouse

'The Pipe-world, Ah'kis, is five thousand miles long and just over ten miles in diameter. It was one of a dozen Arks sent out from Earth to populate distant planets; each meant to journey a mere 200 years at one third light speed. But some accident knocked Ark Six from its course and now 100, 00 years have passed.

'Kassi seeks her brother who has been kidnapped by 'demons' and now travels north to the end of the world. Eighteen months ago she left the City of B'Jing and has now washed up on the northern shores of the circular sea.

'She is accompanied by Sebastian, a sentient bot of dubious origins with whom she can communicate telepathically. That ability seems to set her apart from the rest of the world's population.'

It is rumoured that centuries ago the northern edge of the Circular Sea boarded a vast estuary of verdant green. Wetlands that stretched for a hundred miles fed by the two great northern rivers, Akon and Rydern. Rydern silted up long before living memory, and Akon remains a thin green wavering line in the all-encompassing desert. It was also noxious and undrinkable. The builders of Ah'kis, Ark Six, had developed a water rotation system that was both protective (of cosmic rays) and supportive. That was until the Ark was struck and water began to leak. Slowly the Ark is dying.

Without the delicate balance of numerous systems, this section of Ah'kis has slowly become a desert. A thousand miles of sand with only a smattering of oasis; green clusters around deep wells. It was said that The Spike, the highest structure in all of the pipeworld, had once been surrounded by a jungle so thick that mythical creatures called elephants roamed and the rivers and lakes were full of alligators. Myth and reality have always been uneasy bedfellows on Ah'kis.

At this section of shore, far away from the port of Al Akon, the water foams and roils across a beach that stretches on for a thousand miles. The pale water looks insipid and yellow in the hot midday sun as the sunline shines out without cloud cover. It is as if even those great white whirls of vapour fear to cross this inhospitable stretch of land. The call of gulls echoes about; fiercely penetrating the background swell of water that crashes constantly upon the wet smooth sand. Counterwise, shimmering through the sunline lies the port its squat white buildings foreshortened at this angle. A map more than a city. A curve of geometrical shapes washed out by the sharp sunline.

With no tides so to speak the water is a reaction to all the life within. Every movement echoing outwards to become these random events; these waves reaching out towards the far north before slipping back. One such wave, no bigger nor smaller than the rest, carries a shape. Dark and sodden. The object rolls, pushed by the wave first one way and then another. More waves come to disturb its rest, and just when it seems inevitable that it would be dragged back into the depths, the shape stirs and coughs.

The woman unfolded stiffly. Unsure how long she

has been on land. Uncertain how long she had been not on land at all. She turned onto her back and looking upwards at nothing, contemplated all that had gone before with a dark flatness that bordered on despair. She was naked but for a loin cloth and a sheathed broadsword, her skin glistening with salt, dark from a life spent out of doors for the most part. Her hair was long and tied back. She held onto a cloth bag, now the only thing that remained of her past.

All dead.

Everyone.

Because of those red bastards. Demons, she still couldn't bring herself to call them aliens; and in truth it mattered little. Alien. Demon. Devil. Evil. Whatever they were they had brought her nothing but heartache. First her brother and then Sebastian and Johan.

And the rest.

Her friends. Her lover; her lovers! Fyonne had been slaughtered by them also. And Sin, still a child.

All dead.

Kassi all but contemplated joining them. At times during the night at sea she had almost willed her body to sink, but some other force, some other need, had driven her to keep afloat. To stay alive despite all that had happened. Kirk had warned her, had she not, and as usual Kassi had been stubborn, unwilling to be pushed into something she found abhorrent. Even to save her brother. Gods! Kaze. What was she to do? Alone with a thousand miles of desert between her and any sort of existence; any chance of survival.

There were sounds from behind. Dunes rose, their peaks a swirling mass of dust devils twisting in the stiff breeze that spiralled off the ocean. She should stay here, she thought wearily. The sounds registered as battle. Cries interspaced with the sharp clink of steel on steel.

She should stay here and just rot. Fade away. Give up.

The sounds began to wane, the cries less exhorting, more despondent. Other guttural voices raised in triumph.

Kassi sighed. When was she ever going to learn?

She rolled onto her front and slowly climbed the dune immediately behind her. At its summit she saw a scene at once recognisable and yet strange. Men, merchants by the flabbiness of their bodies and the willingness they had to fall on their knees, had been set upon by bandits. A dozen perhaps. As almost always the merchants outnumbered the fighters, but had no inclination to fight and so were the easier prey. All played out in garb she thought more suited for the bedroom of a tart or princeling. One bandit, obviously their leader just by sheer force of colour and dress sense, grabbed a young boy by his head scarf, and voices were raised. Whatever the merchants had said was obviously displeasing to the man who casually slit the boy's throat.

Up until then Kassi had been equivocal; after all she had done this past eighteen months upon the Circular Sea; how else could she be? But she had never slit any throats.

The bandits rounded the merchants up and took them and their freaky horse things—why did they have lumps on their backs?—and left. When the coast was clear Kassi scrambled across the boiling sand to the boy. He looked nothing like Sin. Although he was dusky and black haired like Sin was... had been, this youth was stout and full of face. His eyes were a deep blue although they held nothing now. Empty of life. Already flies had gathered.

Kassi felt no remorse as she searched the boy's body. She had been at sea for at least a day. No food, no water. She had seen worse times but not by much. What she needed more was fluids.

"Sorry, lad," she muttered before taking her sword and slitting the lad's arm. She slurped eagerly at the trickle of blood. Then she took his head scarf and tied it around her own head. None of his clothes would fit but at present that would not be a problem. At night the temperature would drop but by then she would either have joined Sebastian or be resting by the warmth of a fire.

She waited.

The sunline faded into the moonline; casting a pale light across the desert. The bandits had travelled clockwise away from Al Akon, its port and company of soldiers. They had set up camp and were rowdily enjoying some of the caravan's wares. Specifically its consignment of wine. Inwardly Kassi tutted. Never let your men at the alcohol, not all at once. Train them in discipline so that each man will be willing to wait until a safe location. The desert was not a safe location; she was about to show them.

She had a bow but was not a natural archer. At best she could hit the side of a barn. Fortunately the bandits had kindly sat—well, technically, chained was a better word—the merchants outside and were mostly in the very large tent at the centre of the camp. As far as Kassi could tell, a very large tent was almost by definition the side of a barn.

She lit the flotsam she had found and was

pleasantly surprised to see it actually flare into life. Kassi pulled back on the string, leant upwards. And released. An arc of flame scored the blackness briefly before landing on the tent. She fired four times more before someone noticed the rather lovely flames now jittering across the tent roof. She put her bow down and picked up her sword.

She was wearing the black armour Sebastian had brought her all those months ago in the City[1]. One benefit was the way it appeared to absorb light, especially at night. She stood, unsteadily, and carefully walked towards the camp.

Raised voices had given way to screaming and panic. The main tent was now a beacon with flames a hundred feet tall. In the dry desert everything burnt. Men included. Shadows passed before the brilliant light, casting shades that danced to their own tune. A man ran, his back a mat of flame. Kassi could not tell if he screamed; his voice was lost in the pandemonium.

She silently stepped up to the merchants and cut the first free, handing him her knife and telling him to free the others and run. Without waiting for a reply she strolled into the chaos; a shadow unlike any other that night.

Two men saw her, and her sword, and ran out of the camp. Good, she thought. Two less to fight. She dropped her right arm and her shield flickered into life. It was good to know that whoever built it had made it waterproof. Five men came into view amongst the flickering light and shadows and the roiling smoke from the centre of the camp. None of these appeared

---

[1] See *Kassi and the City Day Three* (*Schlock!: Vol 16 Issue 3*)

intimidated by her. Ah, well. It was fun while it lasted.

With a flick the shield rose into the air and curved up and around as though by magic. It bore down on the men, catching three of them unawares and knocking them unconsciousness. A fourth was sent roughly sprawling to the ground. The fifth hesitated and in that moment Kassi was on him, her sword finding his belly with ease. She kicked the fourth man asleep.

The outer shield returned to her. She waited. Exhaustion flooded her body and she knew that she did not have the energy to even stand for much longer. The battle with the demons and the day afloat had drained her of so much. Still there was a bitter sweetness to the situation. She would die doing what she had always done. Standing up for those who had no voice.

The leader, a prancing peacock of a man, stumbled out of the smoke, two men at his side. He spoke but the roar of flames and the emptiness in her own body drowned out his words. Whatever. She shrugged, which had the desired effect. He ordered the two men to kill her. She twirled her sword expertly. Swinging it in arcs before her. A complicated dance that caught the light from the flames and seemed to draw the red light after it. Creating patterns in the smoke between them.

The men hesitated. She smiled, even though through her helmet they would see nothing. Kassi stepped forward, spinning her sword faster. The light became a web of colours. A pattern that appeared to envelop her in a net of brilliant light.

Suddenly she thrust the sword into the sand at her feet and hoped that the three men would not notice just how much she now needed to rest upon it. One of the two lackeys said something and then both turned tail and ran. Kassi sighed. One left. With no energy he would defeat her and regain his bandits. The merchants would again be rounded up. She tried but did not even have the energy to lift her sword up. The shield sat at her arm. She doubted whether she could even raise it to protect herself, let alone send it spinning into the sky to attack. The warrior girded herself for death. At peace with seeing her friends again.

Then there was a flicker of shadow behind the man and a large mace swung into view, crushing his skull as though in slow motion. Brain, blood and bone flew in a perfect arc. The man had a look of surprise that registered about two seconds too late before he fell to the ground, dead. One of the merchants stood there, mace in hand.

Then Kassi collapsed.

She awoke as the sunline was fading. Another day passed without food and yet she felt stronger. Her mouth had a soupy residue and she understood that someone had plied her unconscious body with water and food even as she slept. Forcing it into her dying body.

An old man stood at the door, waiting in anticipation. She saw fear in his eyes. Had they fed a beast who would take their lives? Despite saving them the merchants had a wariness that came from centuries of experience.

She tried to speak. "Th... thank you. The boy. . ."

"We found him, buried. You have our thanks for that and last night." The old man sat. "I am Gerall."

"Kassi."

"Well, lass. I am glad the Builders chose to send you to our aid."

"What did those men want?" she asked.

The old man sighed heavily. "What does any man like them wish? An easier life. The paths through the desert are known only to those of our guild. We know which oasis will be flowing and when." Others had gathered at the tent flap and there were murmurs of thanks.

"We had thought them from the Shadow Queen herself."

At the name Kassi winced. "Why?"

"'Twere rumours the bitch was coming ashore about here. An' when them bandits came we thoughts us dead; dinnae we, Gerall?"

The older man calmed the younger lad down. "I believe that our guest is in need of rest, Young Perall."

"You can rest easy. The Shadow Queen won't be coming ashore. She's dead," Kassi called out after the youth.

Gerall looked at her inquisitively. "And you know this how?" he asked.

"Because I was the cause of her death," Kassi answered.

The others nodded and murmured in relief but Kassi saw the older man's gaze fall upon the dark black Teflon armour of hers. He looked her squarely in the eye and nodded. Instantly Kassi knew that he understood. "So I see," was all he would say.

Alone Kassi fretted. Out of the frying pan and into the murky depths. Would Gerall keep his tongue? Could she trust him to do so? Did she really have a choice?

She lay back and contemplated.

All dead. All dead; and yet still she managed to survive.

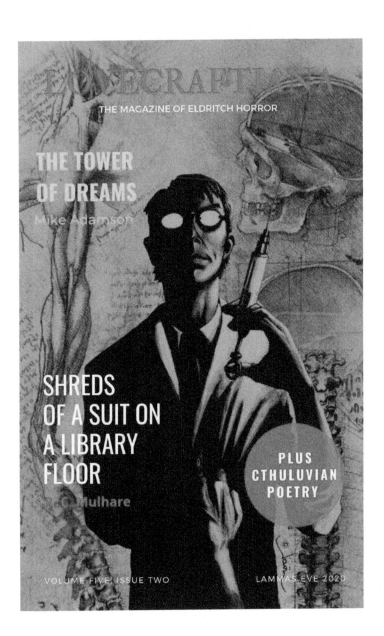

LOVECRAFTIANA
THE MAGAZINE OF ELDRITCH HORROR

THE TOWER
OF DREAMS
Mike Adamson

SHREDS
OF A SUIT ON
A LIBRARY
FLOOR
C. Mulhare

PLUS
CTHULUVIAN
POETRY

VOLUME FIVE, ISSUE TWO   LAMMAS EVE 2020

THE RED CROW by Jon Thomas

I stared out my bedroom window, watching the falling raindrops slide down the fogged up glass. I loved the rain, aside from the splitting headache I usually got from it. Something about the change in barometric pressure. I'm still not quite sure what it is, but it is without fail. Every time it rains, I get a headache. Still, though, the rain relaxes me. The sound of raindrops tapping on my window and falling against the roof of my house really puts me at ease.

It was like any other rainy Seattle day, which doesn't say much because it rains every freaking day in Seattle, but I digress. The gloomy clouds created an overcast in the sky. The perfect weather for napping, so that's just what I did. I laid in bed, tossing and turning, fighting my usual rain induced headache until finally I drifted off.

A loud, incessant tapping stirred me from my sleep. Angry, I shot my head up, flinging my already messy hair around my head even more. I looked around my bedroom, confused at the tapping sound. It wasn't a tapping sound from rain. No, this was loud. Like someone had a stick and they were tapping a loose pane of glass with it.

As I came out of my stupor, I turned my gaze toward the window. I noticed a red shape outside, tapping over and over again, rapidly. I slowly emerged from my bed and darted across my room to my window. Tapping against the glass was a relatively long, narrow bird beak. I wiped the fog from my window and what I saw had me awestruck.

There, sitting on the ledge of my window, in the pouring rain, was a large, bright red crow. As we made eye contact, I noticed a look of either confusion or curiosity cross its face. It turned its head sideways, the way a dog does when it is generally curious, and stared at me for a moment.

I couldn't believe what I was seeing. A crimson crow sat in front of me, staring through beady black eyes into my window and right at me. I guess I should mention that I'm a little bit of a bird nerd. During the summer time, I do some bird watching from time to time. In all my years of being a hobby bird watcher, I have never seen anything like this.

Crows come in one colour, black. There is no variation, they don't have patterns, they are strictly black. Some people call them black birds for that reason alone. There was no doubt in my mind, though. This was a crow, and this crow was blood red. I bolted to my desk to get my phone so I could take a picture of the rare specimen, but upon my return, the crow was gone.

"Damn!" I yelled, frustrated that I wasn't able to get the picture. "I hope it comes back."

Little did I know, I would regret saying those words. In hindsight, I wish that bird had never returned. That bird ruined my life and is the reason I'm writing this from prison. I'm getting ahead of myself, though.

The rest of the lazy weekend went by quickly, with no sign of the bird. I awoke Monday morning, grabbed my usual coffee, Americano with cream and sugar, and headed to work. I worked at a large corporation, the name of which is irrelevant. I worked in accounting, processing payments received and forwarding invoices for outstanding debts to our accounts payable department. It's boring, I know.

My cubicle sat in a corner, butted up to a window that overlooked the Metropolitan area. I was doing my usual, boring paperwork. My eyes were glued to my computer when I began to hear a tapping. I immediately spun around in my swivelling office chair to see that beautiful red crow.

"No way," I said aloud, staring at the bird.

I slowly pulled my phone from my pocket, keeping my eyes fixed on the anomaly in front of me. I swiped the camera app open and, just as I was about to take a picture, I noticed the bird open its mouth.

I expected the thick glass to block any noise from entering into the room. I expected to hear a faint squeak come from outside. I expected anything before what happened next.

The bird appeared to inhale, taking a large breath. Then, it let out a loud, deafening guttural laugh. The sound was not something that would come from a bird. The sound was barely something that would come from a man. Not only that, it pierced my ears through the thick glass. I quickly spun in my chair, expecting to see someone behind me laughing but there was nothing. No one in sight.

I began to feel faint. My vision became spotty until there was nothing but blackness. The sensation of falling in circles overcame me. I became extremely dizzy and suddenly I felt the ground sneak up on me.

When I opened my eyes, I was met with a terrible sight. A surreal landscape of endless sand dunes surrounded me. The sand itself was bright pink and it smelled of sulphur. The sky appeared yellow and the air humid. Really humid.

I looked around, confused at the dreamscape surrounding me.

"What the hell?" I said to myself.

My voice echoed throughout the landscape. Clouds spelled out my words in the sky as they escaped my mouth. I looked up to see giant orange clouds formed into the words "What the hell?"

I began to panic. My feet began to sink into the pink sand and I felt my breath continue to escape me. I began screaming. Calling for help.

"Help me!" I shouted. My words continued forming in giant orange clouds above my head. "Anyone! Please!"

My body began to shake uncontrollably and I felt something wet touch my face. I was slung out of the sand and brought back into reality, quickly.

"Candace!" I heard being shouted from around me. "Candace, wake up!"

I opened my eyes to see a large group of co-workers surrounding me. I was in my cubicle. My face was wet.

"What happened?" I asked, dazed.

My head throbbed. I glanced outside and noticed it was raining.

"We came because you shouted for help!" Brian, my boss, said, exasperated. "We found you passed out on the ground. Are you okay?"

I nodded as I slowly sat up, waving the mass of people away.

"Yeah, I'm fine. Must be low blood sugar," I said, trying to find any excuse to avoid what happened next.

"Okay. Well, official company policy says that we need to call an ambulance," Brian said, jumping to his feet and pulling out his cell phone.

"Brian, ple—" I was cut off.

"Candace, this is non-negotiable." He placed his cell phone up to his ear and walked away from the cubicle.

After a while, the ambulance arrived. They said that the episode was a small seizure and asked that I go to the hospital for a CT scan, to ensure everything was right in my brain. Brian stood by the whole time, giving me no opportunity to refuse any type of treatment. I reluctantly was taken to the hospital.

"So, Miss Rhodes, how are you feeling?" the doctor asked, examining a clipboard.

If I were being completely honest, I was feeling rather uncomfortable. I was completely naked, aside from a sheer hospital gown with no back, and I had just been, basically, forced to go to the hospital against my own will.

"Fine," I replied.

"Have you any history of seizures?" the doctor asked, flipping through his assortment of medical reports on his clipboard.

"No, this would be my first one." I looked down, noticing his shoes.

Don't doctors usually wear comfortable sneakers? I thought.

The doctor must have seen me staring because he quickly explained himself.

"They were a gift," he said, lifting his foot in the air. A gator, or snake, skin loafer sat on his foot. It was hideous. "They're actually much more comfortable than they look." He gave a light, albeit forced, chuckle before moving on. "Alright, your CT came back normal and I don't see any reason for you to be admitted."

I gave an audible sigh of relief.

"However," he continued. "Seizures can have delayed psychological effects. I am going to recommend you see a psychologist, or psychiatrist, for the next few weeks. It's just a precaution, and hopefully nothing will come of it, but we can never be too sure."

He walked toward the door and pulled it open, turning in his tracks.

"Go ahead and get dressed. Once you're done, see Janet at the front desk. She will take care of your out-processing, give you that referral for a psych and take care of your work note."

As he left and the door slammed behind him, I felt my blood begin to boil. The last thing I needed to do was see a shrink. I was fine, I felt fine. It was just a freak occurrence. Something in the back of my mind told me otherwise, though. All I could see was that bird opening its mouth and spewing out that horrible laughter. It didn't make sense. Maybe I did need a shrink.

I got my note from Janet and headed back to work. Immediately, upon my arrival, I was called into Brian's office.

"So," he started, clapping his hands together. "What did the doctor say?"

I handed him the note. "He wants me to see a shrink," I said blandly.

He read the note for a moment, before handing it back to me. How he could understand anything that was written on that note was beyond me. Doctor's handwriting is impossible. He told me to take the rest of the day, paid, and find a psychologist. I resisted at first, but he persisted.

I stood waiting for the bus, browsing the internet, searching for local psychologists. The bus arrived shortly after and I boarded. I sat towards the back and continued browsing the web. Then I heard something next to me. It sounded like flapping of some sort. I averted my gaze from my phone and saw something that sent chills down my spine.

In the seat next to me was a large, red crow. It stood on the seat, flapping its wings and lightly hopping around. I felt the blood leave my face as the bird stopped moving and slowly turned its head toward me. It stared for a moment before slowly opening its beak. I felt tears well up in my eyes and quickly put my hands over my ears.

What came next was both expected and unexpected. The bird let out a blood curdling laugh. A maniacal belly laugh, as if it just revealed a sinister plot to Batman. I screamed loudly, but the people around me didn't acknowledge. People on buses act like weirdos all the time, this was no different. They probably thought I was on something.

The room began to spin and once again I felt a strong sensation, as if I was falling. I awoke abruptly, smashing into the bright pink, sulphuric smelling sand. I jumped up, flinging sand in every direction, and quickly began yelling.

"Help!" I shouted. As the words left my mouth they were, once again, painted in bright orange clouds among the dull yellow sky. "Please, someone!" The echo was unbearable.

The sand began to swallow me once again. This time, there was no one to wake me up. The sand sucked me under. I felt my chest collapsing, I couldn't catch my breath. I began to suffocate and then, I was awake.

It was dark outside, and a small Asian man stood in front of me, kicking my leg.

"Hey," he yelled, "last stop. Gotta go!"

I looked around for a moment, confused. Had I been on that bus all day? I left work at 2 in the afternoon and it was dark now.

I looked at the driver and felt my blood begin to boil. My face heated up as anger clouded my mind. I blacked out. When I came to, I was standing over the small man's lifeless corpse. People stood outside of the bus, staring in shock and screaming. I looked at my hands, unsure of what was going on or where I was. I was holding something. It was flat and squishy. It felt moist. A closer look revealed to me that it was the bus driver's face. I had torn it clean off.

The police arrived, taking me away. The evidence against me was excruciating. The video surveillance on the bus showed me stand up and attack that man, viciously tearing his face from his body. It was a quick trial. The jury had no trouble reaching a verdict and now, as I said before, I'm writing this from the Washington Corrections Centre for Women.

I wish I knew what that bird did to me, what it meant. I still black out sometimes and when I come to, I've done something heinous. I found a shank, carved out of a toothbrush, under my mattress last week. It was covered in dried blood... not my own. Cliché, I know, but it's the truth.

I've seen that crow a few times since I've been here, I think it likes me now. It hasn't let out that unnerving laugh, nor has it sent me back to that terrifying hellscape.

Although I do return there sometimes, when I dream. It's always the same. I'm drowning in a sea of pink sand, unable to dig my way up.

NO MAN'S LAND by Rab Foster

For hours the lieutenant sat on a bench and watched the soldiers come up the road from the hollow where the morning's battle had taken place. He felt no urge to get off the bench and move himself. Nonetheless, he dreaded the moment when a retreating soldier might draw level with him, stop, point a finger and scream: "Coward!"

The worst possibility was that his company captain, who'd looked after him like a father, would limp into view. He'd be limping because the last time the lieutenant had seen him, a piece of flak had ripped open his leg. He'd have every right to stop in front of the bench and scream: "Coward!"

The bench was next to a gateway opening into the grounds of an abandoned chateau, in which the surgeons had set up a field hospital that morning. At some point a gunner wearing only boots, trousers and braces had wandered out through the gateway and sat beside him on the bench. The gunner's torso and face were blackened with powder and above his eyebrows his head was covered with a red-stained bandage.

Though it'd been decades since the chateau was last occupied, the gunner had found a wooden puppet belonging to a child who'd lived there. The puppet was a representation of a soldier dressed in a hussar's helmet and jacket, and was still marked with shreds of scarlet paint. The gunner bent forward, worked its strings and made it march to and fro in front of his boots. At the same time pained, croaking sounds came out of him.

Eventually the lieutenant recognised these as words and he realised the gunner was doing a strangled imitation of a parade-ground sergeant. "Left right... Left right... Attention... About turn... Left right..."

None of the soldiers coming up the road moved like they were on a parade ground. Indeed, as more of them passed the chateau gates during the afternoon, their movements degenerated. The first soldiers ran. Later ones limped and stumbled. The final ones crawled. By the end of the afternoon the lieutenant was watching the last of the crawlers. A soldier dragged himself to a point on the roadside opposite their bench, succumbed to exhaustion and lay against the ground with his head turned towards them. By now the road was so bloody that its dirt had become a burgundy-coloured mud and the soldier's face sank into it. Despite the mud, the lieutenant recognised the soldier as a private in his platoon. Here finally was someone who could point a finger and scream at him: "Coward!"

But even if the dying private recognised him, he wasn't going to scream anything. Something, perhaps a spray of grapeshot, had caught the soldier's jawbone and torn it from the bottom of his face. His jaw and the tongue within it were lying behind on the battlefield.

The lieutenant was still watching the private's face and the crazed gunner was still playing with the puppet-soldier when solid shot began to smash down near the chateau. The surgeons had already fled from the building, in a fleet of medical wagons that'd gone rolling along the road in the same direction as the retreating army. They'd taken with them any injured soldiers whom they'd considered save-able. Now the only people remaining in the chateau were the mortally wounded, who'd been abandoned in its makeshift wards.

Accordingly, a few despairing cries would go up

inside the building every time a distant bang and a shriek in the air announced that another projectile was coming down.

The lieutenant ignored the sounds. He paid attention only to the wrecked face of his platoon-soldier in the mud across the road. Again and again he relived that moment when he'd turned and run and left his men to fend for themselves in the hollow, the moment that ensured he was still alive while the others in the platoon, including the soldier across the road, were dead.

It was only the sound of two horses galloping up and stopping in front of the gateway that disturbed the lieutenant's meditations and made him raise his head. The horses weren't heading out of the hollow but towards it. The first one bore a rider while the second had bags and cases strapped to its flanks. To the lieutenant's surprise, the rider was a civilian, a young, slim man in a frock coat, breeches and mud-smeared boots. His face was shaded by a tricorne, around whose brim a huge red feather curled like a serpent.

"Your battle today," said the rider, "is lost."

The lieutenant ignored him and fixed his gaze again on the dead soldier across the road. The rider turned in his saddle, took in the grotesque condition of the soldier's face and then turned back to the lieutenant.

"Very pretty," he said. "But if you're still looking for excitement... after the excitement you've already had today... I need a porter to help me."

"A porter," repeated the lieutenant. There was a flicker of feeling inside him that he recognised as surprise.

"My horses are exhausted. They can't continue any further. Not that they'd want to continue, with the day drawing to a close." The rider leaned forward and added: "You went in there this morning to fight your battle, didn't you? Well, things would've been different if you'd tried to enter during the night. You wouldn't have been able to enter at all. Your animals would've refused to go."

"A porter?" said the lieutenant again. "Carrying things like a servant?"

The rider climbed down, the slimness of his figure showing amid his flapping, oversized frock coat. "Don't take it as an affront to your dignity. I passed your surviving comrades while I rode along the road, and from the look of them I wouldn't say your regiment has much dignity left. From being an officer in that rabble to being a servant with me isn't a great step down in the world."

The lieutenant gestured towards the hollow. "You propose we go back there?"

"Back? I haven't been there yet." The rider began to un-strap his bags from the sides of the second horse, as if the lieutenant had agreed already to carry them for him. "Are you fit to go back?"

The lieutenant thought about it for a moment. "I am," he said.

Suddenly there was a distant clap and then a whistling noise. Another shot streaked down above their heads and again cries came from the dying soldiers in the chateau. The enemy gunners scored their best hit yet. The shot struck the front wall and brought some of it down in a cascade of bricks and dust. In the gap left by the fallen wall the whole of a first-storey room was exposed to the daylight. The chateau suddenly resembled a doll's house with part of its façade removed.

The rider stared past the broken wall into the room. "The nursery," he murmured. "It was an agreeable old room. Such a pity."

When they started down the road, the lieutenant assumed that the vapour filling the sunken region ahead was an accumulation of the day's cannon and rifle-smoke. Only when they entered the vapour did he realise that it was natural. A mist had formed over the ground. Smoke was present within it, however, soiling it with filthy streaks and swirls.

The road and slope gave way to a flat expanse. Though the mist limited visibility to a circle, the lieutenant recognised this as the site in the hollow where his regiment had assembled early in the morning. Here it'd divided into its constituent companies, which had then fanned out across the hollow's floor.

The site looked squalid. Strewn over the muddy ground was a profusion of debris, discarded, dropped or trampled down by fleeing men—tents, flags, blankets, knapsacks, canteens, rifles with broken stocks and bent barrels, hats, waist-belts, bayonets, bugles, cartridge boxes, rations of biscuits and sardines, a scattered set of playing cards. Beneath the debris the mud was endlessly imprinted with men's footprints and horses' hoof prints. Some pointed forward into the hollow, others pointed back towards the road. They were the crisscrossing signatures of an army advancing and an army retreating.

The bodies of men and horses were too many to count. Along one misty edge of the scene the lieutenant even saw four dead mules, wiped out by a single blast of grapeshot. The wagon they'd been pulling had been overturned too. Now, lying in the sea of mud, the toppled wagon and the humped mules resembled a boat being towed by four black porpoises.

Because the young man had dismounted and left his horses behind, the lieutenant couldn't think of him as 'the rider' anymore. He thought of him as 'the stranger' instead. After taking everything in, the stranger demanded, "Where are your opponents? What were you fighting? Ghosts?"

"Their infantry and cavalry are already on the march again. They're moving north, where in a few days they'll meet our main force under Archduke Brennen. But they still have guns on the heights in front of us, firing after the soldiers they've routed." In fact, one of those guns sounded then and its bang was accompanied by a brief yellowy glimmer of light high in the mist.

"So what happened today was only a rehearsal for a bigger event?"

"Yes."

"A costly rehearsal."

The stranger knelt and produced a map and compass from a satchel. While he unfolded part of the map over his knee and set the compass down as levelly as possible on the mud, the lieutenant glanced fearfully into the smoke-smudged mist. He wondered if his claim was correct. Had the enemy soldiers begun their northward march? Could there still be some in the hollow, with orders to dispose of any survivors who hadn't retreated?

And even as he asked himself those questions, he heard a voice issuing orders in the mist behind them. The lieutenant turned in time to see a lone figure come hobbling into view. It was the gunner with the blackened skin and the red-stained bandage on his head. From one of his hands hung the strings connected to the puppet-soldier, which floated a few inches above the ground. The gunner's hand jerked so that the puppet's limbs cranked back and forth, and he barked at it, "Left right... Left right... Attention... About turn... Left right..."

Untroubled by the gunner's appearance, the stranger folded the map again and rose from the ground. "So," he said, "there's three of us now." Then he removed the compass from the mud, pocketed it and pointed into an area of the mist. "We have to go that way."

"Northeast," said the lieutenant.

"Your sense of direction is excellent."

"My company was sent that way this morning."

"Indeed? Did you come across the ruins of a chapel? Roofless? Walls partly fallen?"

"Yes. My captain told me to secure those ruins with my platoon."

"Ah, a happy coincidence! And did you notice anything of interest there?"

The lieutenant shook his head. "We were fighting a battle, not making a tour of the local landmarks."

The ground changed soon after they resumed walking. No longer was there only mud, churned by galloping hooves and running feet. Now clumps of grass and weeds gave way beneath them, retreating treacherously into the earth with an oozing and gurgling that showed the presence of subterranean water. Because of the weight of the bags on their shoulders, their feet sank even further than they should have done.

There was surface water too, filling the depressions in the hollow's floor. These ranged from nicks and pocks a few feet long or wide to channels that meandered and ponds that stretched for many yards. The water was dark, oily and still and the depressions containing it looked like wounds that'd festered and turned rotten.

As they waded across the viscous black water of a channel, the lieutenant said to the stranger, "I hope your map prepared you better for this than our maps did. We came here expecting dry ground. The cartographers of this region said nothing about a marsh."

The stranger replied, "That's because there wasn't a marsh here before. Not until twenty years ago. Then the owner of the chateau back along the road started an engineering project. He diverted two local streams and sent them down into this hollow, to join a third stream that flowed through the middle of it. And he built a dam to the south. His plan was to turn the hollow into a lake. Unfortunately, instead of getting a lake, he got the morass that we're crossing now."

"Twenty years ago? I thought the chateau had been abandoned earlier."

"It looks like it's stood empty for a long time, doesn't it? But that's typical here. What's new soon becomes old. What's youthful gets consumed. Everything quickly ends up corrupt and decayed."

Before the lieutenant had time to ask what he meant by this, the stranger added, "It's said his attempt to create a lake here was the ruin of the chateau's master. The marsh he ended up with cost him and his family their lives. They died from fevers that they'd contracted from its foul waters." His tone had become rueful. "Well, that's what they say."

They scrambled up the far side of the channel, its black, muddy bank shifting and sliding beneath them so that they almost fell back into the water. At the same time the gunner limped from the mist nearby, still working the puppet and drilling it with orders. He must have found a way around the channel because he hadn't a patch of wetness on him. Despite his madness, the gunner was the most adept of them at traversing the marsh.

In the battle's aftermath, bodies lay amid the grass and weeds and blood latticed the slimy banks as it worked its way down to the pools and channels. Also, bodies bobbed in the water, their faces, hands, uniforms and haversacks already looking as black and putrid as it did.

Near to them now, a field gun lay overturned at the edge of a pool. One side of its carriage and one pair of its wheels were sunk into the bank, while the end of its barrel rested in the grass at the top. Two horses' carcasses, still tethered to the gun by lengths of chain, floated in the water below. The bodies of the gun's crew were strewn on the ground, in the water and down the mud forming the boundary between them. The scene told a story that'd happened many times that morning. Teams of men had been moving the field guns through the marsh and had become stuck. While they struggled to free their guns, the enemy got into positions to rake the hollow with cannon-shot and bullets. Then they were slaughtered.

The lieutenant saw one corpse lying alongside the stricken gun, its feet pointing up the bank and its head… He wondered for a moment if the dead soldier had been decapitated because he could see no head, but then realised that the corpse's shoulders were at the very bottom of the bank and the head was submerged in the rancid water. And then the lieutenant saw something flutter in the water under the dead soldier's shoulders, around where his head would be. Something pale and fan-like…

The body slid down the bank and disappeared piece by piece into the water, shoulders, torso, legs and feet. The water rippled over the ends of its boots and became still again. The lieutenant stared at the pool. Could he see a red stain now, spreading on the surface?

Suddenly he realised that he was being left behind. The stranger hadn't stopped walking and the gunner hobbled behind him, and both were fading into the mist. Not wanting to be alone, the lieutenant hurried after them. He thought about the pale fan-shaped thing he'd seen by the submerged head and the only thing he could equate it to was a hand.

When he caught up with his two companions, the mist ahead was puzzlingly bright. The brightness couldn't be sunlight because it was evening-time now and the sun was departing the sky. Nor could the lieutenant attribute it to the enemy's artillery. It was continual rather than flashing and there were no bangs accompanying it. Besides, he assumed that by now all the enemy's forces were heading north, for their confrontation with the Archduke.

The mist began to glow in hues of yellow and orange, and it shimmered too as if those hues were moving. The stranger looked at him for an explanation and he sifted through his memories of the morning, incoherent though those memories were.

Finally, he said, "My company reached a less marshy area. Where there were trees, ferns, brambles, dry grass… But the bastards were waiting for us. They hammered us. Hit us with such a bombardment it was like hellfire raining down. No wonder the undergrowth ignited and burned."

"Was that where the ruined chapel was?"

The lieutenant struggled to remember. "Not quite. But it was close."

"I wonder if I've wasted my time coming today. Maybe the fire's done the job for me. Maybe it's consumed them." Slowly the stranger turned around, surveying the landscape of mist, marsh and carnage. He seemed to listen for something and so the lieutenant listened too. After a few moments he heard movement beyond the small circle of visibility imposed by the mist. He heard water slapping and mud oozing as things passed through them. And there were other sounds, soft mewing ones made by animals of some type. Their mewing had a note in it that suggested pleasure and the lieutenant asked himself what would make animals feel happy.

Food, obviously. In the mist, creatures that'd been hungry before were feeding.

"No," said the stranger, "they aren't hiding around that old chapel, in danger of going up in flames with it because they're waiting for the sun to set. The mist's shielded them from the sunlight and they've ventured out already. And there's a feast for them today, a glorious banquet laid on by providence!" The stranger started walking again, towards the flames. "Still, that chapel's where we have to go."

A little later they found the chapel and the lieutenant's recollections proved to be correct. It was close to, but not on, the drier ground that was ablaze. The marsh's pools, channels and saturated turf had held the fire back from it. However, just beyond its furthest walls, leaping flames and swirling smoke gave the ruins an infernal backdrop.

The broken walls of the chapel's nave, transept and ambulatory still traced the shape of a cross. They entered it and walked on flagstones that were carpeted with weeds, moss and black marsh-ooze. Above, the glow from the fire etched the jagged tops of the walls in yellow and orange. Attracted by this, the gunner went to an almost-fallen section of wall, scrambled on top of it and climbed up a ridge that rose gradually to a peak about fifteen feet high. There he stopped, crouched, dangled the puppet in the air before him and worked its strings to make it dance grotesquely. His outline became etched in the fiery colours too and he suddenly resembled a stone gargoyle mounted on the wall.

Meanwhile, the stranger led the lieutenant to a block of stone that'd once formed the base of a baptismal font. He removed the bags from the lieutenant's shoulders and his own shoulders and placed them on the block. Then he took out their contents, which included a lantern, a crowbar with a curved, barbed end, a bundle of iron stakes, a hammer and a crossbow. The wood of the crossbow's tiller was smooth and gleamed with varnish, showing that it wasn't an antique but a recent product of a weapons workshop.

"Thank you," said the stranger. "I wouldn't have got here so quickly if I'd had to carry this on my own. You may leave now." But then, ominously, he added, "You may not get very far."

The lieutenant noted the delicacy of the stranger's face. He was used to the rough pugnacious countenances of soldiers and this gentle face didn't belong to someone who'd enter a battlefield armed with a crossbow. "Who are you?" he demanded. "What's this mission of yours?"

"I assume you know the history of this place, this scrap of land that so many of your comrades died fighting for today. How many times has it changed hands over the centuries?"

"Well, before we marched in here, our commanders told us a dozen different armies had seized it at different times."

"A dozen at least. Maybe more. My father distinguished himself fighting under Archduke Brennen's father on the second-last occasion that it changed hands. And because that campaign was a success, my father was given an estate in the region as a reward. At the heart of the estate was the chateau where I met you this afternoon." Again his tone became rueful. "Some reward. More like a curse. It wasn't long after my father took up residence in the chateau that the visits began. Nocturnal visits made by his new neighbours, who lived down in this hollow. Visits that invariably ended in deaths... Our guards and servants first... Their bodies emptied of blood..."

The stranger sighed and for the first time the lieutenant sensed desperation in him. "I've heard plenty of lore about how to fight these creatures. The trouble is, I don't know what to believe." He lifted the bundle of stakes. "These, for instance. Some say that if you hammer them into their hearts... But my father was told they could be destroyed by water. That's why he tried to turn this place into a lake, to drown them. Well, he didn't make a lake. He made a marsh, but a marsh still contains water and that doesn't seem to have stopped them at all." He paused. Mewing sounds could be heard over the crackling flames. "Listen to them feasting. I think they like this watery hellhole that my father created.

"I was the youngest child and he sent me to live with my grandparents in the capital before I became another victim. And after I left, my family died too. My mother, my brothers, finally my father himself. Not from marsh fevers as some people have claimed. They were slain by the horrors that dwell here.

"Unfortunately, when I was old enough to understand what'd happened to my family, old enough to swear revenge, I couldn't get back into this region. Our friends in the east had launched a counterattack and pushed the old Archduke's forces west again, behind the line of the former border. This meant for years it was impossible for me to return to my old home, especially because my family name was bound up with the cause of the Archduke. If I'd set foot here and the occupiers discovered my identity, they'd have put a noose round my neck.

"But when the young Archduke embarked on this new crusade, to reclaim these eastern lands that'd belonged once to his father... I saw my opportunity. I'd ride in behind your army. It didn't matter who the ultimate victor was. I knew the area would be in such confusion that I'd have time to get to this chapel and strike."

"And what's at this chapel?"

"A few members of my father's household survived the onslaught. Once, I tracked down his old valet. He told me that just before my father died, he became convinced that the source of the evil was to be found here. Supposedly this chapel contains a crypt. Long ago, when this was a functioning place of worship, the crypt belonged to the family who originally built the chateau. But at some point, the crypt was commandeered."

"By whom?"

"By the chief of the brood. It's beyond my powers to destroy all of them, but if I can destroy her…" The stranger moved away from the block of the font. He started probing at the ground with the crowbar, as if hunting for a loose flagstone that might be prised up like a trapdoor. His parting words were: "Maybe by knocking out the high command I can disable the army. I'm sure that's what your military tacticians would advise."

Left alone, the lieutenant looked around and began to see evidence that soldiers, members of his platoon, had been in the ruins that morning. The soiled flagstones were marked with imprints of boots. He saw debris too—a dropped hat, a discarded bayonet, an abandoned haversack whose pockets bulged because the army-ration biscuits in them were soaked and swollen with marsh-water. And on the ground at the far end of the ruins, in a section that might once have accommodated a chapel choir, he spotted a slash of flickering red. Something metallic lay there, reflecting the glow of the fire outside. He approached it and discovered a tasselled sword.

It resembled the sword he'd carried into battle that morning, which he'd lost at the same moment he'd lost his nerve. The lieutenant picked up the sword, wondering if it was his.

Meanwhile, the remnants of the wall forming the chapel's eastern end rose no higher than his waist and the fire raged not far beyond it. A couple of trees stood amid the conflagration, their trunks and branches reduced to black spindles. His gaze shifted from the sword to the scene outside as he became aware that other figures were visible besides the skeletal ones of the trees.

Three or four of them squatted before the flames while at the same time edging backwards. Their skins were smeared with marsh-slime that glistened in the firelight. From their heads sprouted wreaths of hair that looked little different from the tangled clumps of grass and weeds that the lieutenant had trudged through earlier. Their angular bodies, gaunt limbs, splayed hands and tapering fingers suggested marsh creatures like lizards, frogs or wading birds that'd grown to impossible sizes. Now, as they crept back on their haunches, from the fire, towards the chapel, he could see that they were dragging things with them.

The lieutenant realised they were pulling soldiers' corpses, whose blood they wished to feed on before the fire consumed them. Unable to stop himself, he exclaimed: "God!"

One of the figures turned its head. Its features were impossible to make out because of the riotous, Medusa-like tresses of hair surrounding them. Only the eyes were discernible, shining as two points of light. For a moment, their light was a bright yellow. Then, imitating the changing flame-colours in the background, it became orange. And then it took on other colours, red, blue, green and…

The light in the creature's eyes became a glinting icy white and suddenly the lieutenant no longer felt afraid. His fear gave way to numbness and apathy.

Abandoning the corpses they were dragging, the creatures swivelled and came scrabbling towards the chapel on flat, wide hands and feet. Still inexplicably lethargic, the lieutenant stood and watched them approach.

Then, dimly, he heard a voice up on a wall behind him. "Left right..." raved the gunner as he played with the puppet. "About turn... Left right... Halt!"

Hearing those parade-ground orders reminded the lieutenant that he was a soldier, one who'd been in a battle. In turn, this reminded him that he was at the site of the battle again, which brought back his awareness of the horrors approaching now. His fear returned too. With the creatures only a few yards away, he turned and ran.

He fled along the length of the chapel and out of its far end, into the marshland that he'd crossed earlier. The evening had darkened and whatever visibility had existed in the daytime mist was gone. After a minute of running he careered into a pool that he hadn't seen in the gloom. He ploughed through water and mud and somehow managed to get across the pool and out of it, but then lost his balance and fell flat.

As he lay on the ground, he realised that there was a body lying just in front of him. Its face was close to his. After a time, when the lieutenant's eyes had adjusted better to the darkness, it occurred to him that the face's mouth had opened and its eyelids had risen. The body was a living one rather than a corpse.

Then words emerged from it. "Who... Who's there?"

He recognised the voice as that of his company's captain and dull-wittedly he replied: "It's me."

"Lieutenant?"

"Yes."

"I'm injured, lieutenant, badly injured. Got it in the leg. Can't feel a thing there. Don't have any idea how long I've been lying here. What's happening? I can't hear any rifles or artillery. How has the day gone? Where do we stand?"

"We... We put them to flight, sir." He thought for a moment and added, "Yes, we fought our way up those heights to the east and knocked out their field guns. After that it was simple. The scoundrels we didn't kill or capture have already run halfway home."

There was a note of satisfaction amid the pain in the captain's voice. "That's good to know, lieutenant... I think now I can die contented."

From behind the captain came a splashing noise and a splayed shape pounced out of the darkness and landed on one of his legs. The captain began to slide away. Scrambling onto his feet, the lieutenant saw that another channel oozed past on the far side of where the captain was lying. From its torpid water stretched two arms that ended in long-fingered claws. These grabbed at the captain's uniform, hopping from the legs of his blood-soaked breeches to his belt and then to his tunic. As the claws moved, they reeled him over the channel's edge and into the water.

"No!" spluttered the lieutenant. He realised he still clutched the tasselled sword and he swung it at the arms. With his free hand he seized the collar of the captain's tunic. By now only the older man's head and shoulders remained above the channel's oily surface.

A second pair of claws burst out of the water and grasped at the lieutenant's legs and he hacked at them too. Meanwhile, one of the first claws fastened onto the captain's hair, tore him free from the lieutenant and dragged him completely beneath the water.

A moment later the lieutenant's sword struck the second attacker. He felt liquid spatter his face and the claws released him. In fact, one claw dropped from the end of its arm and rolled along the ground by the channel's edge. Then, briefly, something thrashed in the water. When the thrashing subsided, the lieutenant saw two points of light glaring up at him from the channel, turning red, blue, yellow, finally white. He experienced the same strange lethargy that'd transfixed him in the chapel, but then the white points dimmed and melted away and he was free again.

He thought of the captain and moaned, "I couldn't do things right this morning. I can't do things right now!"

But then he remembered the stranger and realised he had one last opportunity to redeem himself. He ran back to the ruins.

As the lieutenant re-entered the chapel, he saw the gunner still perched on top of the wall, absorbed in making the puppet dance in mid-air before him. He was unaware of a figure that advanced towards him along the wall-ridge, moving on all its limbs like a huge spider.

"Look out!" yelled the lieutenant. "Look out!"

The gunner gave no sign of hearing and continued to play with the puppet. After another moment, the creature reached him. Gaunt arms enclosed him, a small black mouth puckered towards his throat and his face vanished amid tendrils of hair. Unable to watch, the lieutenant dropped his gaze from the wall to the ground. He saw a line of scarlet blotches appear across the flagstones as blood jetted out and fell from fifteen feet above. Then the puppet landed on the flagstones too. Its head and limbs snapped away from its torso so that the only things holding it together were its strings.

The lieutenant struggled to control himself. He ignored the blood and the broken puppet, looked around and saw how several of the creatures were also moving at ground level, scrabbling towards him from the eastern end of the ruins. And he could hear many more of them. Their mewing sounds came from all sides. In another minute, he imagined, tides of them would invade the chapel from west, north and south as well.

Across the nave he saw a new light, not glimmering and extensive like the firelight but bright and compact. He also heard a voice call, "Lieutenant!" He realised the stranger was waving a lantern and hailing him from a corner where an arm of the transept jutted northwards. The stranger gestured to the wall beside him. A screen of leaves and creepers that'd hung there had been ripped down and dumped in a pile. In the newly exposed stonework was a semi-circular opening about five feet high. The lieutenant ran over. By now, from the eastern part of the chapel at least, the creatures had come so close that he could hear the points of their claws scraping across the flagstones.

The stranger bundled him through the opening and ducked through it himself. Inside, he thumped his lantern on the ground, wrestled a curved wooden door around against the opening and propped his shoulder against it. At the same time, he produced the hammer and an iron stake from his frockcoat. Then he banged the stake into the surface immediately behind the door's edge, into a line of mortar between two blocks, to ensure that the closed door stayed closed.

While the stranger worked, the lieutenant looked through the lantern-light and found himself in a grotto with walls that, like the opening and the door, were curved. The walls arched up on either side and came together in a low, hemispherical ceiling. Long beards of cobwebs, dust and dirt trailed from them. On one side, a hole in the floor revealed the head of a stone staircase that spiralled steeply into the earth, thousands more cobwebs forming a gross fur down the sides of its shaft.

Behind him, the stranger knocked a second stake into the old, crumbling mortar. The crossbow was now strapped across his back.

"Down there?" asked the lieutenant.

"It has to be down there."

After the stranger had secured the door with a third stake, he picked up the lantern and the pair of them descended. They followed the stairs down for five or six revolutions of the staircase but then encountered an expanse of black water that filled the space below them. Slowly, the stranger lowered himself into the water. He stopped when it was as high as his thighs.

"No more stairs," he said. "Floor."

He raised the lantern from the water's surface and they discovered that they were no longer in a stairwell. Rather, the staircase had arrived at the corner of a chamber whose dimensions looked similar to those of the nave above, between the transept and the chapel's western wall. The stranger waded forward and the rays from his lantern reached deeper into the chamber.

Rancid fleeces of dirt and cobwebs covered the ceiling and the upper parts of the walls. The floor and the bottoms of the walls were concealed by water that'd presumably flooded in during the ill-fated project to turn the hollow into a lake. The water had the same repellent oiliness as that lying outside in the marsh. Here, however, the stench that the water exuded was unable to escape and it infected the remaining air. As the lieutenant breathed, he felt he was inhaling poison.

They soon noticed that the water had another unappealing feature. "What's this?" the stranger asked and picked something out of it. The lieutenant, who'd waded into the water behind him, saw that he was holding a glistening black cord. On either side of his fingers, it sloped down into the water again.

The lieutenant looked about in the lantern-light and realised that these cords covered the flood in the chamber. They lay across it like an unravelling carpet. "Maybe it's marsh-weed?"

The stranger rubbed the cord between his thumb and forefinger and the lieutenant saw it break into many thinner fibres. "This isn't weed we're moving through," he said. Then he dropped the cord and motioned for the lieutenant to take the lantern from him. When both his hands were free, the stranger removed the crossbow from his back and turned its crank, drawing the bowstring along its tiller.

While the stranger worked at the crossbow, the lieutenant noticed that in the chamber's centre a patch of water had begun to glow. He pushed towards it, gripping his sword-hilt in one hand and the lantern in the other. He realised he was approaching a submerged light and, though it was obscured by the water, the light had colours. One colour would dominate for a moment and then give way to another, red, green, yellow…

Still priming the crossbow, the stranger barked behind him: "Don't go any further!"

But already the lieutenant had reached the light. Looking down, he saw there were in fact two lights, radiating from the eyes of a pallid face that was suspended a few inches beneath the water. Then, suddenly, the face rose and broke through the surface.

Under the face a body emerged too. At the same time the lieutenant felt things writhing around him. As the figure ascended, the black cords slithered up from the water. They snaked up the figure's sides, enclosing its body like a stringy cloak and finally crowding together on top of its head, where their ends were rooted in its scalp...

Her body, her head, her scalp, for he realised he was looking at a woman. Floating on the floodwater had been countless tresses of this woman's hair.

He raised his sword but suddenly the colour burning in the woman's eyes became icily white. The apathy that'd afflicted him earlier took hold again. His arm dropped and the sword-blade dipped into the water. He heard the stranger shout, "Don't look at her eyes! She can suck out our souls as well as your blood!" But by then it was too late.

Too late, reflected the lieutenant. The thought was like a weary sigh.

White light still seeping from her eyes, the woman turned her head towards where the stranger was standing. She spoke. "You too! Look at me!" Just as her eyes contained many colours, so her voice seemed to be a dozen voices combined. It sounded male and female, young and old, high pitched and deep, musical and guttural. At the voice's core, however, was something that suggested the coldness of an Arctic wind. "Look at me! You must look!"

The lieutenant heard the bolt hiss free from the crossbow, but it missed the woman by several feet and flew uselessly into a distant corner. At the last moment, evidently, the stranger had looked into the icy light and fallen captive as well. "Good," said the woman. "Good! Now, my dear, come here. Come to me!"

The stranger waded into the edge of the lieutenant's vision. He still held the crossbow but his arms hung limp and it trailed through the water beside him. "That's it, my dear, come closer," the woman urged. "I think I'll deal with you first."

She reached out and knocked away the stranger's tricorne so that for the first time the head of hair underneath was revealed. Then her hand began to caress the stranger's face. Her own features changed. Her mouth puckered forward, her lips forming an O-shape. Needle-like fangs slid into view all around the O's circumference. And a long, thin tongue, hollow like the proboscis of an insect, flicked out from between the fangs and swished about the circled lips.

Yet it wasn't this grotesque transformation that startled the lieutenant from his trance. It was the sight of the stranger's long blonde hair spilling out from under the tricorne that allowed him to escape the creature's spell. Suddenly he understood why the stranger's clothes had seemed so oversized, the stranger's figure had seemed so slim and the stranger's face had seemed so un-masculine. He lifted his sword out of the water. Seeing this, the creature shifted her gaze back to him, wanting to transfix him again with the polar light. But by then the lieutenant had raised his sword in front of his face, across his eyes.

He saw the white light flare along the blade's edges and then the creature gave a pained cry.

As he drew the sword back behind his head, he saw how the creature's eyes had become grey and dim. Perhaps the steel blade had acted like a mirror and channelled the freezing light back to its source. Not hesitating, he swung the sword in a massive arc. When it struck the creature's neck, it sheared through hair, skin, tissue and bone almost as effortlessly as it'd sheared through the chamber's foul air.

Later, when he inspected his sword, he found that several tresses of hair were snagged on its blade. The head dangled under the blade at the ends of those tresses. He thought of the gunner's puppet and suddenly he murmured: "Left right... Left right... Attention... About turn... Left right..."

They returned to the grotto at the top of the stairwell. The stranger produced the crowbar with the curved barbs. By positioning the barbs around the heads of the three stakes that she'd hammered into the wall to secure the door, and levering the crowbar back, she could prise them out again.

"We could wait," she said, "till the morning. When daylight's come and they've retreated to their hiding places. They'll be easier to kill when they're asleep."

"And where are their hiding places? Are you sure they're inside these ruins and not outside, amid all that water and mud? How will we ever find them when they're nesting across a whole marsh?"

"So you're willing to go out now?"

The lieutenant raised his bloody sword. "They're monsters but they're not indestructible. I could kill some of them at least. Probably more than we could hope to kill during the daytime."

The stranger contemplated him. "You ran away from the battle this morning, didn't you? You didn't want to run but running was what happened. Am I right?"

He didn't answer.

"I sensed it. The first time I saw you, I knew you were someone who'd suffered the way I had. Everyone around me, everyone dear to me died, and yet I escaped. Not that I'd wanted to escape. I'd rather have died with them. And the guilt of not dying has tortured me every day since."

It was a long time before the lieutenant said anything, and then he spoke briefly: "I'd better go out now."

"Yes. We'd better go out."

They began to remove the stakes.

HYPERBOREAN BOOKS

WITCH-QUEEN OF THE LOST RACE

by Rex Mundy

RED-HEADS by Joseph Farley

Nadja was a red head, but her pubic hair was blue. Combined with her pale white skin, she came off as patriotic.

"Come back to bed," she called.

Robert Ledmer slid onto the sheet and lay down beside her. He turned on his side and grinned at Nadja. "I bet you are a blond under all that colour."

She laughed, showing perfect teeth. "You'll never know."

"I can find out. I can shave you while you're asleep, then wait to see what colour grows in, though it might take a few days."

Nadja pinched his nose. "You touch my hair and I'll kill you."

"I won't touch your head. Just down below."

"I might let you do it, just for the surprise you will get."

"What surprise?"

"My pubes will come back blue."

"Blue?"

"My hair is dyed red. Otherwise it would be blue."

Robert thought about this. "Blue can't be your natural colour."

She nodded, "It's not natural."

"What do you mean?"

"I spent two years on Malik, back in my Peace Corp days."

Malik. Robert had heard about the place. One of the small worlds orbiting a nearby star. The USA and other nations had been colonizing it for the past twenty years. It was a dry rock covered planet with roasting days and freezing nights, but it had what mattered most—liquid water underground and a passable atmosphere.

"I've been to Titan," he said, "but my hair is the same colour it always was."

"It's a dietary thing," Nadja explained. "There's not a lot to eat on Malik except for the local fare. I sort of got hooked on Stygian worms."

Robert put his arm around her.

"I've heard of Stygian worms," he said. "Space crews bring a canister with them for emergency rations."

Nadja confirmed this.

"The worms are high in nutrients, protein and calories. You only need to eat one a day to survive."

"I've never had one. What do they taste like?"

She shrugged, "More or less like you might think a worm would taste, except some added spice, like tabasco sauce. That comes from the head. The worms are blue, but the head is small and red. They cut off the heads on the worms packed for space rations. That's so the crews can still think clearly, and other reasons, but mostly for logical thinking. The ship owners don't want any of their crews acting odd with their investments. A distress signal can be received, and a crash can be salvaged."

"Hallucinogenic?" Robert guessed. "Now you've made me interested. Maybe I should give them a try."

Nadja shook her head.

"It's a high like no other, but I wouldn't recommend it."

"Why not?"

"I told you, I am a little hooked—a bit addicted."

"To Stygian worms?"

Nadja rolled onto her back, and tugged the sheets up over her stomach.

"Yes, the heads are highly addictive," she said to the ceiling. "Two years on Malik will do that to a gal. Malik gets old five minutes after you leave the landing craft. A few Stygian worm heads and you can dream you are anywhere, or dream that the dud you are with is your favourite movie heartthrob."

Robert looked at his body. "How many worm heads have you eaten today?"

"Just one. I try to pace myself because of the side effects."

"The blue hair? That's not so bad. It sets you apart."

"I can live with that. There are worse side effects."

"Such as?"

Nadja turned her head towards her temporary paramour, and explained.

"The sex organs of Stygian worms are in their heads, and the heads can breed even after separation from the body. It is how they evolved. It's their survival strategy. Get eaten, then multiply. The heads digest slowly. Eggs can be spit out and fertilized in your stomach even with all that churning acid. Then, sooner or later, you have baby worms. They grow very slow and eat very little, at least for the first few weeks. But, with time, that changes."

"What do they eat?"

"Guess."

The thoughts of Nadja being nibbled away did not sit well with Robert.

"Have you been tested for these worms?" he asked. "There has to be a cure."

"Of course there is a cure, but it only works half the time. I get tested every month. Still, the odds are against me."

"You could stop eating the stuff," Robert suggested.

"Tried. Dozens of times. When I say I am a little bit of an addict, that means I am alive. If I was a big addict, eating two of three worm heads at a time, I'd be dead in a week. I might not even know it. I could just drift from life into death while absorbed in one never ending fantasy. I could be near death now and not know it. I could be in excruciating pain, but not feel it because my mind is telling me I am having the time of my life."

"I'll pass then."

"Pass on what?"

"Stygian worms. I won't give them a try."

Nadja stroked his face. "Smart boy."

They lay in bed. Robert dozed with Nadja in his arms. He dreamed of a far off planet. Nothing but rocks and dull provincial colonists. There was nothing to do, day after day, except work, sleep, eat, and try not to die. One day he was offered a red dot, a worm head. A free sample. He had nothing better to do at the time. The next moment he was in the best dream he had ever had. Breath-taking, vast expanses of colour, worlds to be explored and experienced. People, creatures, stories, lives. Then he woke. Nadja was gone. He was alone in the bed. He glanced at the back of his hand, and saw fine blue hairs growing there.

HYPERBOREAN BOOKS

THE
FOREST
GOD

by Rex Mundy

AT THE EDGE OF THE UNIVERSE: A FILLING
STATION by Mason Yates

Art wandered the candy section of the filling station, trying to keep his head low so that other customers did not have to catch a glimpse of the inky black eye on his face. Though, the real reason for hanging his head was so that he did not have to face the embarrassment of being caught with a black eye. If someone asked about it, he wondered what he would say. He got into a bar fight last night? He tripped and fell down a flight of stairs? No, he didn't want to come off as being a washed up drunk or a clumsy fool. However, he knew he could not tell anyone the real reason for the dark, swollen eye. He wondered how people would react to hearing that his wife punched him after finding him in bed with another woman. He winced at the thought.

He gave his head a little shake and came out of his thoughts, returning his attention to the sugary substances on the shelves in front of him. On his way to his sister's house, a place where he could stay until everything in his life calmed down, he decided to pull over at a filling station to buy his nephew a candy bar and a pack of cigarettes for himself. He needed the nicotine, and he guessed buying his sister's son a candy bar would qualify as an act of appreciation for letting him stay a few nights. He grabbed a Hershey's bar and looked at it. Who didn't like Hershey's?

For a quick moment, he looked around, seeing a few other people wandering the aisles, then stepped away from the candy section and made for the front counter. He hoped he could grab a pack of Pall Malls, pay, and get back to his red pickup truck outside before anyone could question him on his eye. One thing he knew about small town people was that they could be nosy, very nosy. The last thing he wanted was to run into a curious bastard who had to know everything in the universe. With his head low, he approached the counter and started to fish in his pocket for his wallet, telling the cashier he wanted a pack of Pall Malls while he did so.

He hated the thought of returning to a bad habit, but he needed something to calm his nerves. Within the last twenty-four hours, everything had gone to hell in a handbasket.

Before he could bring the wallet out of his pocket, a loud screeching sound caused him to turn his head to the front of the building. He caught a faint glimpse of a large cloud of orange and an assortment of vehicles in the sunlit parking lot, then the windows at the front of the station imploded. Small pieces of glass, as small as individual grains of sugar, flew in every direction, showering everyone inside. For a few milliseconds, he felt the shards cut into his skin and engrain themselves inside him, then a blast of heat pushed him to the ground. A sudden blackness engulfed his vision.

He wiped the dust off his face, then slowly opened his eyes. From his position on the ground, he discovered that the filling station appeared to be normal, as if no explosion had taken place. The windows at the front of store were intact, and the items on the shelves were fully stocked and positioned precisely, almost as if he had walked into a perfectly placed movie set. He glanced at the front counter and noticed nobody on the other side. He swung his head to look down the aisles, expecting to see a person or two, but nobody stood there either. He sighed and returned his focus to the front windows. Looking again, he noticed something different about the outside world. Instead of daylight, he noticed it was dark. But that wasn't the only thing different. The whole world—the cars, the trees in the distance, the roads leading to the station—had vanished.

He quickly stood up to get a better view. On his feet, he realized nothing existed outside the boundary lines of the filling station. The parking lot and the gas pumps were still there, everything held together by a large slab of concrete. He estimated the concrete island he inhabited was about a hundred yards wide and maybe a hundred and fifty long. Past the concrete, nothing existed but an infinite blackness, a void.

He walked to the front of the station and put his hands on the window, gazing at his surroundings with his jaw hung loose. From the inside of the station, he examined the edge of the concrete island. If he fell off the edge of the island, would he continue to fall forever? He imagined himself descending into an infinite abyss.

He backed away from the window. He couldn't continue to think about that. The thought ate at his mind.

"Hello?" he said in a raspy voice. "Hello? Anyone here?"

His words bounced off the filling station's walls. Nobody returned his shouts.

"Dammit," he cursed and gazed around the inside of the station. Shelves full of food sat motionless in the middle of the store, and refrigerators full of refreshments were positioned by the walls. On one end of the building, he saw a few shelves with small bottles of basic medicine, and on the other end, he saw a few items for vehicles, including a couple jugs of oil and an assortment of tools. By glancing around at what he saw available, he realized he would never go hungry or thirsty on the concrete island, and if for some reason, he couldn't take the loneliness, he could either swallow a handful of pills or drink a few jugs of oil to end his suffering. He hated to think that way, but given the bizarre situation he found himself in, he could not exclude those options.

He sighed again and returned his ponderings to where exactly he was. He remembered being in a filling station when something—an explosion, he guessed—had ripped through the station and landed him on his ass. He remembered the heat, and he remembered shards of glass sprinkling his skin. Remembering that faint detail, he looked down at his arms and legs. There were no cuts, and he didn't feel burned by the searing heat he once felt.

Then, a thought: maybe he had been flung into a dream?

He pinched himself. Nothing happened. He shook his head. "Nope," he said to himself.

He returned to his inner thoughts, searching the labyrinth of his mind for any ideas that could explain the situation he found himself in, but nothing came to the surface. As he mused, he glanced around the interior of the building. Vivid memories of being tossed to the floor accompanied looking around, but no explanation occurred.

But something else did. Outside the filling station, beyond the concrete island, headlights approached.

Art opened the filling station's glass door and stumbled onto the walkway in front of the store. He did not go any farther. He only wanted to go outside and wait to see what the approaching car had to offer. He watched for a moment as the lights grew closer and closer. The vehicle acted as if it were travelling on a highway in a straight line, but as far as Art could tell, there was no highway, only a deep blackness. Perhaps, he thought, somewhere out there a road could be found, but nothing was within sight of the filling station and the concrete island.

As the lights came onto the island, Art could finally tell what sort of vehicle approached, a small blue BMW with an Indiana license plate. The windows were tinted, blocking his view of the driver, but Art already knew who the car belonged to—his wife. Upon seeing the blue body and the emblem on the hood of the car, he almost collapsed to the ground. A chill raced through his veins, and sweat beaded his forehead. He took a step back, leaning his body against the front windows of the filling station. He eagerly watched as the car parked next to a gas pump. He hoped someone else would step out of the car. He desperately wanted to see his wife again someday, but he didn't want to see her on the concrete island. He also felt like it was too soon to see her. However, he rethought, maybe she had answers to where they were.

With this new idea on the forefront of his mind, he took a step forward, eager to see if his wife actually stepped out of the car. He gazed at the vehicle, his heart thumping madly in his chest. For the first time since landing on the concrete island, his eye started to throb again. Sweat trickled down his face, and his body produced a strange heat within him. He hated to be held waiting.

"Honey?" he asked in a shout. "Honey, is that you?"

A strange moment of silence passed before the car door opened and his wife stepped out. Her blonde hair fell to her shoulders, and a smile stretched across her face. Another oddity of seeing her was the clothes she wore: sparkling high heels, a tight and short blue dress, and a pair of aviators shielding her eyes, though Art had no idea what she would need to cover her eyes from in the dark expanse.

"What are you doing here, babe?"

"Searching for you," she responded in that voice he knew and loved. He almost expected his wife to have an alien voice.

"Where am I?" he asked, stepping off the walkway at the front of the building and walking across the concrete island to his wife. She neared him, too.

"You're in a special place," she told him, taking off her aviators. Blue-green eyes stared at Art as he neared. "You're in a place where reality meets the afterlife. A middle point."

"What happened to me?" he asked. "How did I end up here? I... I was in a... filling station. I... I'm still at a filling station."

"This," his wife said, indicating the filling station on the concrete island, "is where you were knocked unconscious and put into a coma. A woman tried to commit suicide by running into the gas pumps. The whole place went up in an explosion. You're in a hospital now."

"In a coma?" Art asked in disbelief. "Hospital?"

"You're lying on a bed, and I'm standing over you, trying to forgive and forget what you did to me."

"You're not actually my wife, are you? You're somebody else. I'm sorry for what I did to her."

His wife—or a version of his wife—smiled. Her eyes analysed him, searched him up and down for a lie. She gazed into his eyes, piercing him and searching for the truth. Her smile grew wider.

"You're correct," she said. "I'm not really her, but I'm a piece of her. A spiritual piece of her that is here with you. Here with the man that cheated on her."

"It won't happen again," he said. He edged closer to her. "I swear it won't happen again. I regret everything. I regret it. I wish I could take it back. Is this place some sort of purgatory? Am I being detained for my wrongdoings?"

"In a way." She shrugged and took a step closer to Art. She grabbed his hands. "You need to do the right thing from now on. Your wife loves you."

"Who are you?" he asked. "I don't understand. What did you mean when you said, 'a spiritual piece of her'?"

She stood in front of him in silence for a moment, her smile growing wider and wider with the passing of every second.

"Want to take a ride?" she asked, cocking her head to indicate the BMW. "I'll take you back to her. You can tell her you're sorry yourself."

"Am I leaving this place?" he asked, looking around at the dark void.

"If you want to," she said. "Unless you need to wait here a little more and think about things. Maybe that's what you need. Should I come back?"

"No," Art said immediately. Shaking his head, he repeated, "No."

"Then get in, Art. We're going back to the real world. We're leaving this filling station at the edge of the universe."

Art did not question anymore. All he wanted was to leave the lonesome concrete island and get back to his wife. He needed to get back to reality and apologize, but he needed to do more than apologize. He needed to make things right. Getting into the blue car, he tried to think of all the ways he would change things, all the ways he would show his wife she was the only one in the universe, the only one for him, the only one he loved.

The spiritual body of his wife started the car. Together, they left the concrete island.

The light blinded him. Thoughts of being in Heaven surged through his mind, then he saw the figures standing over him. His eyes blinked open. The throbbing in his face no longer felt confined to his eye, but instead, his whole face hurt. He felt like a truck had collided with him. For a desperate moment, he wanted to return to the concrete island where pain felt almost non-existent, then the figures over him became visible. On one side of him, a doctor wearing blue clothing. On the other side, his wife. Her blue-green eyes gazed down at him. Her mouth hung open as if in disbelief that he had woken up from his coma. Tears emerged from her eyes and streamed down her cheeks. She laughed, a celebratory laugh it seemed

He felt himself smile.

"I'm sorry," he whispered. He was unable to say anything louder. "I'm so, so sorry."

THE FLORENTINE VAMPIRE: LOVE IS THE DRUG THAT KILLS YOU by Francis-Marie de Châtillon

Chapter 6.

When all this started I was Guy de Nanterre and I was married to my beautiful wife Othenin de Villefranche. I was the lord of Nanterre, a rich man but not overly opulent in my life-style. Pious? Of course. A true believer? Yes. And in love? Oh yes, yes! I'd gone off to Crusade as was expected and found the situation one of great alarm. The Mussulmen, by the 1170s, were uniting against us and Saladin began expanding his power from Egypt and had started to surround the Holy Land. The result? The Kingdom of Jerusalem was being encircled by a unified enemy for the first time in its history. Saladin attacked the Crusader state in 1177 but King Baldwin saw him off at the Battle of Montgisard. In the wake of the battle we had an uneasy truce. And with it, as the Mussulman states were uniting, there was increasing tension and argument in Jerusalem. Then Guy de Lusignan came to the throne in 1186. He was supported by a Raynald de Chatillon, a loose cannon if ever there was one. Raynald—I knew him well—attacked any trade caravan he could, provoked Saladin on every occasion and turned his castle at Kerak into a pleasure dome. In saying all this, he was also a very competent military commander and not a bad man really, in my opinion. In any event things came to a head when his men assaulted an especially large trade caravan, and in the fighting his troops killed many of the guards, captured the merchants, and stole the goods.

Well of course. Normal. Now Saladin, operating within the terms of the truce, sent envoys to Guy seeking compensation and redress. Reliant on Raynald to maintain his power, Guy was forced to send them away unsatisfied. This meant war. To the north, Raymond of Tripoli elected to conclude a separate peace with Saladin to protect his lands. This was a mistake and he shouldn't have done it. The deal backfired on him when Saladin requested permission for his son, Al-Afdal, to lead a force through Raymond's lands. See the problem? Raymond saw 7,000 men enter Galilee and defeat a Crusader force at Cresson on May 1st. Guy got windy and called his allies to assemble. He hoped to strike before Saladin could invade in force. Raymond renounced his treaty with Saladin and joined Guy and a Crusader army of around 20,000 men near Acre. I was in that army with my two hundred or so men. Advancing, we occupied a strong position near the springs at Sephoria.

Possessing a force nearly the size of Saladin's, we had defeated earlier invasions by holding strong positions with reliable water sources while allowing the heat to cripple the enemy. It was a good tactic and one we owe to Raynald. Saladin sought to lure us away from Sephoria so that we could be defeated in open battle. To do this, he personally led an attack against Raymond of Tripoli's fortress at Tiberias on July 2nd while his main army remained at Kafr Sabt. That night, we commanders held a war council to determine our course of action. While the majority was for pressing on to Tiberias, Raymond argued for remaining in the position at Sephoria, even if it meant losing his fortress. Guy, a hasty man prone to jump at his own shadow, elected to push on in the morning. Marching out on July 3rd, our vanguard was led by Raymond, the main army was led by Guy. Balian (a manipulative bastard at best) had the rear along with Raynald and I and the military orders. We moved slowly as we were under constant harassment by Saladin's cavalry. I remember reaching the springs at Turan six miles away around noon. It was blisteringly hot and we needed water badly. And this is where it all went tits up. Though Tiberias was still nine miles away, with no reliable water en route, Guy insisted on pressing on that afternoon. Under increasing attacks from Saladin's men, we reached a plain by the twin hills of the Horns of Hattin by mid-afternoon. Advancing with his main body, Saladin began attacking in force and ordered the wings of his army to sweep around us. They surrounded our thirsty men and cut off our line of retreat back to the springs at Turan. Under increasing pressure we, the rear-guard, was forced to halt and give battle. This stopped the entire army's advance. And now you'll see Guy for what he was. Though advised to fight on to reach Tiberias and water, he decided to halt the advance for the night. We were surrounded by the enemy and possessed one dry well. Got it? One dry well! The next morning we awoke to blinding smoke. Saladin had set fires to screen their actions and increase our misery. Guy broke camp and ordered an advance towards the springs of Hattin. But despite having sufficient numbers to break through the Mussulmen lines, fatigue and thirst badly weakened us. We were in the shit, as they say.

We advanced and Saladin counter attacked. Two charges by Raymond saw him break through the enemy lines, but once outside the Mussulman perimeter, he lacked enough men to influence the battle. As a result, he retreated from the field. Desperate for water, much of our infantry attempted a similar breakout. It failed. Forced onto the Horns of Hattin, the majority of this force was destroyed. And without infantry support, we trapped knights were unhorsed by Mussulmen archers and forced to fight on foot. We fought long and hard but were driven onto the Horns. It was during one of these fights that I got bitten in a grapple with a Mussulman who just refused to die. I eventually severed his head, but by then it was too late for me. I was infected. And after three charges against the Mussulmen's lines failed, we were forced to surrender. This was on the 4th July, 1187. I shall never forget it. Among those captured were Guy, Raynald, and me. Guy was treated well but Raynald was personally executed by Saladin. I was taken as a prisoner and eventually ransomed by my family. Others were not so lucky. Their families would not pay to get them back. We lost the relic of the True Cross which was sent to Damascus. Saladin then quickly went on to capture Acre, Nablus, Jaffa, Toron, Sidon, Beirut, and Ascalon in rapid succession. Moving against Jerusalem that September, it was surrendered on October 2nd. So there you go! Now you know!

CONTINUES NEXT MONTH

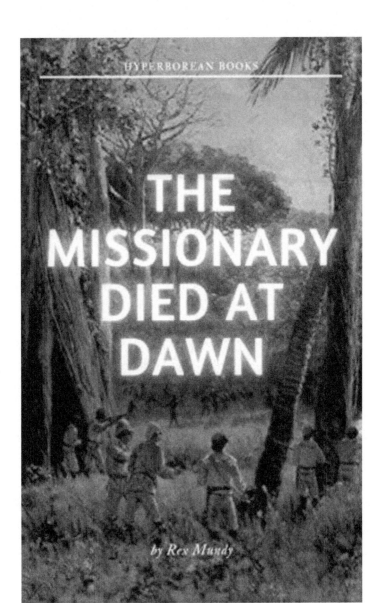

HYPERBOREAN BOOKS

THE
MISSIONARY
DIED AT
DAWN

by Rex Mundy

A REAL JOB (ONE OF THE FEW) by Matt McColum

Ted has never understood what exactly he's been looking at in the mirror. He always sees an outline of a man, and that's as far as it ever goes. He forgot what he really looks like, and really doesn't care anymore, truth be told. He knows other people see things within that outline, but he knows they're just seeing what they want to see. He knows how people tend to be, not much different from him. He just has a little bit more awareness than they do. He'll look down and try seeing what he wants to see, just like the others do, only he just isn't as successful when it comes to doing that with himself.

So Ted will just do what he always does to start his day. He'll shake that outline out of his head, brush the teeth that he can sense but cannot see, take his shower, put on his clothes, and go ahead carrying on with this routine of make believe, instead of giving any real thought to why he even bothers. When he's done Ted will wipe away his doubt, like a five year old wiping a long line of snot off his face. Then it's out the backdoor he goes.

Ted will spend the rest of his day in the middle of the deep woods, which is where his job is, one he hikes about thirty minutes to. It's also a job that he still doesn't really understand. During the hike it takes Ted a while to completely wake up, while his boots crack down on the hard leaves that echo throughout the silent forest, smelling that bittersweet scent of smoke in the morning air, wanting to taste it, being angry that he can't, feeling safe in knowing that there is no forest fire to come, as he asks himself what makes him so special.

It's when Ted knocks on the door of the old, rusty, torn up shed, that he knows his day is about to become something unusual again. It may follow in the same tracks as the other days; however, Ted knows better how different it will really be, from a much deeper point of view, that's hard to put together for him.

"What in the hell do ya want?" shouts Hurley.

"Just open the door, let's get something new going already."

"Alright, fine."

"Hurry up," nags Ted, "I'm starting to get a headache already. I need something new to cure it."

"There ain't none of that for ya," Hurley snaps.

The same old monotonous pain begins to weigh in on Ted.

Hurley opens the thin wet plank of a door, not hiding the disappointment straining his face, in a bitter glare.

"I thought you were my mother at the door, I hadn't seen her for 'bout ten years now. I was really thinkin' it was her."

"My new day has now officially begun," Ted sighs with relief, not fully knowing why.

"Just get in here, let's do what we gotta do."

"You mean what I gotta do. Not you, me! I hate how you always forget that." Ted steps in, just trying to remember all of the money that will later follow, while once again trying not to ask where Hurley gets it from.

Hurley pretends not to hear the complaining, as he drags his bare feet through the dirt floor at every heavy step, ignoring all of the mosquitos planting itchy bumps all over the bulbous muscles on arms, which doesn't fit well with the plump beer belly he waddles around.

Hurley's empty, darkened shrine of a home always keeps his principles in line whenever he gives it a good look around, he doesn't care for what the others consider to be "the good life"; there's just too much dishonesty in it, by his definition. They both walk through the darkness, Ted wondering where the cold breeze is suddenly coming from. Usually he sweats so much that he finds himself wondering how Hurley doesn't dehydrate in that oven roasting darkness. He'll notice a few drops of sweat on the top of that bald head of his, but it seems like he should be drowning in sweat with this being Hurley's home. Sometimes Ted will go numb walking through the deserted shack, he'll tell himself it comes from newly arrived bug bites, from bugs he assumes scientists haven't discovered yet, even when Ted secretly knows why the numbness is really in effect. Something he always becomes dumb to as the days go on. Ted suddenly feels the stairs steering him downward, then upward, without a chance to give it much notice.

When the bright white light hits him, Ted hears Hurley yelling, "Come and get 'em, kiddos!"

That's when Ted feels bolts of energy blasting into him from every which way. He feels movements from all sorts of living organisms squirming around in all directions inside of him. In ways they feel faded, almost as though the sensations are only there to tease him.

Ted closes his eyes and tries to see this, hoping this will be his lucky day, but it isn't. All he sees is the same old blackness staring back at him. He can hear the usual, which is really just more of the unusual. Nothing is ever the same when it comes to what he hears. This time he hears screaming and hollering inside himself, he hears chanting and moaning, followed by the roaring of gigantic beasts, then the chiming of heavenly bells. His body vibrates, then he begins to feel overcrowded. This part is the only part that is actually common in this process.

Eyes appear all over Ted's body and he stares into a silver waterfall all around him. He is knee-deep in mud, doused in blood. Chopped up organs crawl around him the way bugs would. That's when hands of all shapes, all sizes, all colours, all textures, shoot out from the waterfalls and poke out random eyes with their index fingers, until one hand finally reaches into him, before the other ones can, pulling him in its direction. Like always, this happens too quickly for Ted to see which hand made it in. All he knows is there he goes, same as always. When he hits the silver water he finds himself in another place.

The tunnel is bright blue, stripped down to the pure energy that makes it what it is. This is how Ted has always viewed it, to where a strong voice is injected into him to reassure Ted of the materialized nudity. Small children in the nude peek out and ask Ted if he can guide them back home.

"I don't know where home is really. Not just yours, I don't even know where mine is."

"Please don't lie, mister, it isn't welcome here," pleads a little blond girl with bright blue eyes. Ted feels as though they are bloodshot, no matter how clear they seem.

Ted notices all of the children mesmerized by something on his stomach, like it's letting out a bright ray of light in various alien colours. When Ted looks down he sees nothing, just the blue tunnel beneath his outline. Ted wonders if there is a screen on his stomach, with many trapped and directionless worlds behind it, and perhaps he's just blind to it, because he swore off ties to most sections of the outside, many moons ago. Ted suddenly gets the feeling that what they are looking at isn't on his stomach, but actually inside of him.

"What is it? What's in there? Don't tell me I'm pregnant, ha ha."

"No," answers a little boy coldly, with a large scar on his forehead, one that crawls around the way a centipede would in a closed jar. "They have already grown, aeons ago. So have the worlds they have brought with them."

"What are you talking about, kid?"

"They're all over the world, sir. Just like all of the others are all over the world."

"Who?" Ted asks, now in strong urgency.

"Can you take me home, please?"

"Who were you talking about, kid? Who is all over the world? Why don't we know about them?" Ted feels as though he is about to do something to this young boy that he may regret later down the road.

"You know about them, sir. That's all that matters. You don't know about them when you don't want to, and don't need to anyways then."

"Really?" Ted now felt relieved, though not quite knowing why exactly.

"Sir, take me home now, please. Please take us all home."

Before Ted can respond he feels himself being dragged away by a powerful force. Just a brief delay was all.

Everything goes blue and Ted can feel layers of what he thinks may be his skin rolling around, like a forgotten burrito in its plastic wrapping, bouncing around for weeks in the backseat of some slacker kid's car, without ever being noticed.

"I'm trying to pretend I can sleep! Knock it off, will ya?" Ted hears in himself.

"Who are you? What are you?" is all Ted can let out.

"Someone who likes to pretend they are one of the very few who can actually sleep, so I won't have to perform tasks every moment of my existence. Is that really so much to ask?" is all Ted gets from whoever is inside him.

"That sure was some answer." Ted's sarcasm made an astounding swan dive in mid-air.

"Well, I certainly am the lazy type. Odd you haven't picked up on that yet. I mean with you and I connected. I thought you would be the cosy type, I was semi right about that," the voice responds, as though being a wise-ass is what it needs for breathing purposes.

"Where am I? If you're not going to answer my other questions then can you at least answer that one?"

"You've been here before. Try asking me new questions for once. This was cute at first, but it gets old as the centuries fly by."

"Centuries?" Ted chuckles. "I've only been doing this for a few months now. Oh wait, you're being sarcastic. Well duh, I should have seen that coming."

"Actually no, I'm not joking or being sarcastic or whatever you want to call it. You haven't been coming here for only a few months. Neither has it been that way with any of your other stops. I can't blame you for thinking that, though. I should have expected it really. I guess the Hallow Man would have been wrong for picking you otherwise."

"The Hallow Man?" Ted exclaims, "Who is the Hallow Man exactly?"

"That so called human being you call "Hurly". We just call him the Hallow Man for our own personal amusement, it's a joke that only us here would understand. Speaking of the word personally I find the word human to be an insult for the Hallow Man. He deserves better. I know, they always tell me, he still has to perform his duties no matter how degrading they may be. I'm just saying…"

"Being a human is degrading in your eyes?" Ted tries to hide the side of himself that agrees.

"Well, just the side that he has to indulge in as a human being. I'm not naysaying all of it. Your limitations would surely bury me if I had to carry on with them. On the other side, however, I certainly do see all of the values in having such great lengths in limitations."

"How so?" Ted has got to find out all about this one, so he tells himself.

"Well, if I ruined that limitation for you others would start to fall, and then you would lose that gift. A gift that you need more than any other. Consider what you are as a whole. Something else I can't tell you without robbing you of all your needs. Just think a tad bit more about it, that's all I'm saying."

"Well, thanks, glad I wasted my time with you then." Ted's sarcasm was beginning to gag him.

"You didn't waste anything. You will though, if you don't remember to breathe. I mean literally breathe, right now!"

Ted breathes in the suffocation, spreading its massive weight all around, deep within. So Ted breathes, with all suffocation being locked away for another day.

As soon as that realization catches up with him, so do the colours change all around him.

Colours and shapes of all types form around Ted, ones that he is not familiar with, but it feels as though they are familiar with him. They all dance around and distract Ted as spirits from all spiritual worlds tear into him. He feels none of this, it tingles a little, scratches a little less. No blood is to be seen, not even dry wounds can be seen.

Ted begins to wonder what he is standing on. He looks down and sees a fuzzy, bright orange glow. He wonders why it isn't burning his feet. He feels some sort of movement at the pit of his stomach, he feels things being taken out of him from various areas inside. "What do you want?" Ted screams.

Worlds launch out of the eggs that had been dumped inside Ted, launch out in powerful beams now. They swirl all around in Ted, in a silver glow, before sprouting into places far beyond any of his perceptions. Ted becomes blind when this happens. So all is black.

Ted knows he's locked in, his feet planted in the soil of a world he knows nothing of. One that is far beyond his sight. He feels something pulling him up. A springing force stretching him outward. A gush of wind and away Ted goes.

He roars out as a demonic humanoid machine, in a world of napalm charred bodies breezing apart by the seconds in an ashy storm, as Ted sinks his claws into two flat children made of tinfoil. One is slightly shorter than the other, neither one affected by the storm. The taller one has to try harder not to crinkle up when Ted transmits pathways that they very much so need in themselves, in order to become three dimensional steel, with built in jetpacks, ready to blast at will. They will be able to go wherever they need to, for whomever they need to, if they can hold up enough of a hunger for it. All they have to do is trust Ted.

They seem to be lacking in trust as they daze outward, as though he isn't even there. That's when Ted finds another pathway in himself, along with others he doesn't know about, with all of the company that a vividly vibrant pathway tends to bring. This crowd is unseen, unfelt, but this never lasts for too long, when it comes to specific senses.

"What is going on?" Ted asks the silver fog that shifts all around him. As it clears up Ted can see a crowd, very similar to what lives inside himself. Their hideous appearance is something he isn't strong enough to handle, diseases in a living figuration that make it abundantly clear why diseases in general are automatically set for destruction. Ted always manages to run into these kinds of entities no matter how they dress themselves. As Ted stares intently, just as they do, while the falling of patience takes place on both ends, he knows that he has just entered the exit of his journey, one that must always be both temporary and endless. He knows that whatever they decide to do with him is what's best, something he has been sure of the moment he began, many moons ago.

Later in the day, Hurley spends hours digging up pieces of Ted's ceramic body. He polishes up the pieces the best he can behind his broken shed of a home, with the cleanest towel he can find. After a while he glues them back together with the cheapest glue he has. Then places the body in a bonfire, a little farther out back, right where the rest of the forest meets up. Smoke fills all of the forest real fast, much of it comes from faraway places that are often unseen and unheard, far beyond a simple bonfire. The bonfire only gives off a very small portion of that smoke, the rest of it is just there to mingle. The bonfire portion of the smoke will part ways and find its way home. It will later make its way right back to the shack, the very next day, without much memory, but a strong urgency to get paid. The rest of the smoke will later fade from view, gliding around hectically in its invisible frustration, since adapting to a foreign environment often calls for much pain, anguish, and confusion, in a traditional misplacement such as this.

Shadows Along The Road.

Josef Desade

Schlock! Publications

Printed in Great Britain
by Amazon